(DELPHINE PUBLICATIONS Presents)

Pieces of JUSTICE

A NOVEL BY *Saundra*

AUTHOR OF *HER SWEETEST REVENGE*

D1372995

Pieces of Justice
Delphine Publications focuses on bringing a reality
check to the genre urban literature. All stories are a
work of fiction from the authors and are not meant to
depict, or represent any particular person.
Names, characters, places, and incidents are either the
product of the author's imagination or are used
fictitiously, and any resemblances to an actual person
living or dead are entirely coincidental.

Pieces of Justice
© 2013 Saundra

ISBN 13 - 978-0988709386

Published by Delphine Publications
Edited by D.P. Stingley
Cover Art by Odd Ball Designs
Layout by Write On Promotions
www.DelphinePublications.com
Printed in the United States of America

Dedication

For my Mom and Sister. I love you!

Acknowledgments

First I want to give God the glory, honor, and praise because he is the head of my life. Thank you God for blessing me with the knowledge of creativity I love it. I want to take some time to tell my husband how much I appreciate him for taking this literary journey with me. Well Mr. Jones I thank you sooo much from the bottom of my heart for traveling with me, cooking dinner for me, and the kids on days that you have worked a twelve hour shift, just so that I can write on my next project. I want you to know that I appreciate it and it does not go unnoticed. I LOVE YOU!! I want to thank my mom, dad, sisters (Angelia&Saidah) and my brothers for supporting me at all times. To Mary my stepmother who I have always thought of as my mom also, because she loves me and treats me as one of her own. I love you! Quatesha my crazy friend I want to congratulate you again for graduating this year 2012 and receiving your RN degree I'm so proud of you.WEW!! I have to show love to my daughters DJ & CJ the most important part of my life. Mommy love you two!!

Tamika Newhouse my publisher who took a chance on me Thank You I'm loving this literary world. As for the whole DP family let's keep writing that Hot Urban Fiction we are making our mark. Shout out too all my friends and family I want go through a list of names but if you support me than you know who you are. Special shout out to Larissa (I see you). And I always have to thank my sister in law Latunya Jones Ross she is my #1 fan in the family. I love her to pieces. Shout out to FWHA crew Michelle, Nicole, Amy, Trisha, Tiana, Lashawnda, Gay, Denise, and Betty. Shout out to Shawntia Hardaway my new friend who is about to take this Literary World by storm!! Congratulations Shanta on your engagement I'm so excited for you. And get busy because you know that wedding day will be here sooner than you think. I want to give a pre-congratulations to both of my nieces Zaleikia and Corlunda on their 2013 high school graduations. I'm proud of you two and I love You!!

To all my fans I want to THANK YOU Erica Nicks, Deirdra Smith, Arnetta Philpott Hairston, and SelfAssured to name only a few, without you I would not be writing. And I know all of my fans are screaming for a sequel to "Her Sweetest Revenge" stay buckled in your seat belt I gottcha. Now take the time out and read my first romance novel this is a first for me. So take your time reading this and I hope you enjoy. GOD BLESS!!

Author: Saundra Jones
1 Key Stroke At A Tyme!!

Pieces

of

JUSTICE

Chapter One

Waking up with another migraine headache was not the way Justice had planned to begin her morning. She had to be in court in an hour, so getting rid of the pounding headache that was threatening her sanity was a must. She got out of bed, slid her feet into her baby blue silk Prada slippers, and headed straight to her Italian-style bathroom where she grabbed a bottle half-full of Extra Strength Excedrin out of the medicine cabinet. Justice had been taking these pills for the last four months, and she was fed up with it. Especially since her physician had been telling her there was nothing wrong with her. According to her physician, all she needed to do was take a vacation, get a real social life, and relax. In some ways, she understood what her physician was saying, but in other ways, it just seemed absurd. She had spent six years in law school, graduated top of her class, and sat in Starbucks with coffee-crazed people for months to study in order to pass the bar. There was no way she had done all that to lie on some damn beach three months out of the year.

To be perfectly honest with herself, she knew the headaches were coming from the trauma in her life with

Keith. She had finally got over the fact that he had been lying, stringing her along, and promising to marry her, while he was out finding his "true self-worth." This, by the way, was bull. Justice and Keith had dated the entire time they were in law school and not once did she ever pressure him to get married. In fact, it had been Keith who had decided they should move their relationship in that direction after they both had been promoted partners at their firms. "A big step into high society" is what he had called it. The wedding had been planned, arrangements made, and the date set. Then two days before getting the marriage license, she picked up the newspaper to discover that Keith had filed for his marriage license already. But with someone else. Talk about being crushed! She stayed in bed for two weeks crying her eyes out. But with the promise of her career she picked up the pieces and moved on.

All that had been four short months prior. Justice was sure she was over Keith and that whole incident. But the migraine headache she had awakened with this morning was making her contemplate. One thing she was sure of was she had to pull it together because court was calling. And Justice always put her clients first, regardless of personal tribulations.

Ring, ring!

The phone interrupted her thoughts. Justice didn't know who was calling at that hour, but they had not picked a good time.

"Hello," she barked in the phone from pure agitation.

"What took you so long to pick up?" Kiki yelled into the phone.

2

Justice immediately threw her hand to the center of her forehead, which was pounding with aching pain. "I was taking something for this migraine," she responded.

"Oh, I am sorry. I didn't mean to yell," Kiki apologized. "I can't believe you're having another one of those awful headaches. I told you all you need is to have some fun. And I have *just* the thing."

Justice could imagine the grin that was on Kiki's face while she planned something that only she could possibly enjoy.

"What is it this time, Kiki?" Justice already had the words dripping on the edge of her tongue.

"Why do you have to say it like that? Sounds like you already got your mind made up to say no. You could at least find out what it is, first." Kiki sounded offended.

"I didn't say no. Just no more blind dates, OK?" The last two blind dates Kiki had set up for Justice turned out to be complete disasters. And the last guy was the worst. Not only did he still live at home with his mother, his former wife, who he had not yet divorced, lived there too. On top of that, he had his soon-to-be ex-wife drop him off at the restaurant for their first date. As a result, the date was a pure disaster. It turned out Kiki had no idea he was married, but after that, Justice vowed she would never go on another date that Kiki prearranged.

Kiki couldn't believe her ears. All she ever wanted to do was find her cousin a good soul mate. She had no idea that all those guys had so much baggage. "No, it's not a date. You remember my friend Renee? Well, she's having a card game tonight. And I was thinking you could go along. You know, have a few drinks. You might enjoy it."

"I don't know, Kiki," Justice said, sounding unconvinced. "The last time I went to one of your friends' card game, there were a lot of weird people attending. And remember those guys started to fight over the game? I'm a lawyer, Kiki. I defend people accused of second degree murder. I don't stand around and watch it unfold. Especially over a card game."

"Justice, stop making excuses to stay at home and lie on the couch with another deposition file in your hand. Now, I'll be around about 8:00 tonight to pick you up," Kiki stated.

"Uh, I don't know, Kiki." Justice still had not made up her mind. "I'll be at the office late tonight. I have some briefs to go over."

"Justice, you have already put in over eighty hours this week alone. You deserve this," Kiki tried to convince her.

Justice started to relax as she realized her headache had started to ease up while she had been on the phone. "Look, I'll call you later. I have to be in court in an hour," Justice said, still not giving in to Kiki's reasoning.

"All right, just think about it," Kiki asked as she smacked on some gum. Justice could picture Kiki while she was talking on the phone with her. Kiki was probably rubbing her scalp with the tip of her long, colorful, manicured fingernails. She and Justice were first cousins, and they were close. But they were as different as day and night. The only thing they had in common was their Aunt Mattie who had raised them both.

Saundra

Justice had come to live with Aunt Mattie in Gulfport, Mississippi, when her grandmother, who had been raising her, suddenly died. Justice had lived with her grandmother in New York ever since her mother had enlisted in the military. The initial plan was for her grandmother to raise her while her mother was away. However, when her grandmother suddenly died, plans changed. Rachel, Justice's mother, still had two years left in the service where she was stationed in Japan. The military gave her a two-week release to come home and settle her affairs. That's when Justice learned she would be going to live with her aunt Mattie until her mother finished her tour in Japan. But six months after Justice was settled in with Aunt Mattie, a call came that her mother was killed in Japan when a sniper misunderstood a signal she had given. Justice felt her whole world shift to an awkward position; she was only eight years old. But that's also when she decided she would carry on her mother's dream and become a lawyer.

Ever since she had been old enough to remember, that's all her mother talked about—becoming a lawyer. Rachel knew the military would pay for her schooling, and that's why she enlisted in the military. Rachel's love for the law is what forced her to name her first and only daughter, Justice.

Kiki had already lived with their aunt Mattie when Justice came along. Kiki's mother had died while giving birth to her. Kiki was an only child, so she and Justice became close cousins, thick as thieves. Needless to say, Kiki and Aunt Mattie were very concerned about Justice's well-being, especially her love life. Justice tried to explain to them that except for her migraine headaches she was fine. The only dream Justice desired at this point was to become a judge. That was the only place Justice intended to put her time and energy. Her heart was closed to love.

ððð

Austin waited patiently as his daughter Morgan took her precious time talking to her friends as she descended from the school building. He loved her so much, and even though she was twelve years old, he still considered her to be his baby. His only daughter, she had been going through so much lately, yet still seemed to be the perfect kid. So he didn't mind that she took her sweet time talking to her friends knowing that he was sitting there waiting to give her a ride to the YMCA where she was enrolled in swimming lessons.

"Hey, Dad," Morgan said, as soon as she opened the car door and bounced down in the front seat.

"Hey, how was your day?" Austin smiled.

"It was OK. Got a lot of homework, though," Morgan said as she threw her black and pink Nike backpack in the backseat. "Did you hear from Mom today?"

"No," Austin said, easing out of the school parking lot into oncoming traffic.

"Dad . . ." Morgan paused and cleared her throat. "Do you think she's coming back this time?" A single tear slid down her left cheek.

"I don't know. But hey, let's not worry about that. You have so much other stuff you need to focus on."

"Like what? Not drowning?" Morgan grinned. "Don't worry, ad, Coach said I'll be swimming the Red Sea in no time," she joked.

Austin smiled at his daughter. He knew how much she was hurting inside, and he had plans on making it right this time around.

"Dad, it's OK to be sad. I'm sad too. But my mind is made up. I want to stay with you even if she decides to come back. I won't go back. I mean it," Morgan said, matter-of-factly.

Austin pulled in front of the YMCA and unbuckled his seat belt. "Look, I don't want you to worry about anything, OK? I just want you to focus on school and being happy. Promise me."

Morgan unbuckled her seat belt and reached in the backseat to grab her gym bag that had her swimsuit in it. Settling back into the front seat she looked at her father. "I promise. I love you, Dad," Morgan said, then reached over and gave her dad a huge hug. "See ya later." And with **that**, Morgan jumped out of the car and fell into step as she ran into the entrance of the YMCA.

Austin sat back in his seat and took a deep breath. He was sick and tired of Monica running off every time she felt life was weighing her down. Ever since they had split six years earlier, she had been making life a roller coaster for Morgan. One minute she is stable with a job caring for Morgan. The next, she's dropped Morgan off with him and left town for a couple of months. And this was the last straw. He just couldn't take it anymore. No, this time he had decided she could stay gone because with or without her consent he was getting full custody of their only daughter.

Two years ago he had begged her to give him full custody of Morgan. But Monica claimed that his being a homicide detective was too risky for him to be trying to raise a daughter alone. According, to Monica, "he just didn't have the time to love her." He spent too much time away from home was her argument. Austin knew better, though. Monica just wanted to be in control of the situation. She wanted to be able to pop in and out of Morgan's life whenever she pleased. But that was it; he had had enough finally.

Just as Austin pulled away from the curb of the YMCA his cell phone started to vibrate. He hit the TALK button.

"Where are you?" Trent said on the other end of the phone.

"On my way back to the station. I just dropped Morgan off at swimming lessons."

"Well, look, I need you to head down to the courthouse. We need to talk to that DA, Kyle, about that homicide with the Wilkins's father. I talked to his secretary about ten minutes ago. She said he agreed to speak to us for a minute if we meet him there since he has night court. Can you be there?"

"Yeah, I can be there in drive time," Austin said, in his not usual vigorous voice.

"Aye, what's up? You sound bombed."

"I'm cool. Just got some things on my mind, but I'll see you when I get there." Austin hung up the phone. He had been waiting for a while to talk with the DA about the Wilkins's father's case. Tom Wilkins's immediate family had gotten him an expensive lawyer to get him off by reason of insanity. But it was clear there was nothing wrong with the guy other than he wanted to collect on his family insurance

.The thought of the guy made Austin nauseous. He couldn't understand how someone could kill his entire family, then claim to be crazy. But at this point, Austin and Trent just wanted find out where the DA stood on their decision.

Austin raced up the stairs of the courthouse anxious to meet with the DA. Finally he made it to the top and turned right at the corner. Trent waved at Austin to get his attention. Austin threw up his hand. And out of nowhere someone walked smack-dab into him and papers went flying.

"I am so sorry," Justice apologized. "Really sorry."

She looked at Austin for just a brief moment and was instantly smitten. The guy was drop-dead fine. At that moment Keith never existed. This stranger was about 6 feet 2 with a Colgate smile and smear of dark chocolate ready to be eaten. Feeling ridiculous for thinking such thoughts of a complete stranger Justice immediately remembered herself, and went after her papers that had spilled in the hallway.

"It's OK. I was in hurry also."

"Umm, let me help you." Austin stumbled around trying to help pick up the stack of papers that had flown out of Justice's hand on impact. He handed her the papers that he had gathered, and that's when he got a good look at her. She was gorgeous. Her skin was like butter that you spread smoothly across your buttermilk biscuits, and her lips were identical to Angelina Jolie's. Her green eyes were shaped like almonds, and they accented her brown hair that hung loosely at the nap of her neck in a perfectly trimmed wrap. There was no doubt about it. She was mixed with something, but it was clear she was still a black beauty.

Justice accepted the papers from Austin, happy that he had helped retrieve them but anxious to be on her way and out of his presence. "Thanks. Again, I'm sorry." With that, she continued down the hallway and stopped in front of the elevator. Austin's mind had been so jumbled when he entered the building that he never considered the elevator. He gave Justice one last glance before he heard Trent call his name. He had forgotten all about his reason for being at the courthouse. And he knew he would never see her again.

Chapter Two

Justice didn't understand why she sometimes had to sit in court and listen to well educated attorneys like Clay make an ass out of themselves. She knew that Clay was aware that there were no grounds for his client's case, but Clay appeared to be fighting hard to make his point. Judge Madison had the look on his face that Justice felt inside. *Clay and his client are both full of it.* Naomi Green, Justice's client, had been fired because she kept turning down the sexual advances her employer had been making at her. But since he couldn't openly fire her for that he fired her for tardiness. *How childish,* was Justice's first thought when she was presented with this case. Now that they were in the courtroom, Clay kept going on and on about how "Naomi had been late on numerous occasions" and quite frankly, it was becoming extremely annoying to Justice.

"Your Honor, may we approach?" Justice said, as soon as Clay finished questioning one of his witnesses.

"Approach," Judge Madison said.

"Your Honor, I think this charade has gone on long enough. All Council has to do is convince his client to settle so that Ms. Green can receive her complete benefit package. No less." Justice stood her ground.

"Your Honor, I advise this is not a charade but rather a justifiable reason of why Ms. Green didn't receive nor was offered a benefit package. And I can assure you this is not out of character for the company after an employee is fired, rather than retire or resign."

"Council, you should advise your client that if he doesn't drop this charade, my client will be suing him for sexual harassment and a list of other harassment charges. And I can assure you . . ." Justice looked Clay directly in the eyes, "that will cost him more than a benefit package and an exit resignation," Justice threatened with a smile.

"Is that a threat?" Clay adjusted his tie, trying to hide the defeat on his face.

"Councils . . ." Judge Madison gave them both a warning look.

"Your Honor, I advise Council to go back and discuss this with his client before we proceed any further. It would be in the best interest of his client. I have nothing further, Your Honor." Justice rested her case.

"Well, I advise that you both remember who you are addressing when you come up to this podium," Judge Madison warned them again. "Step back," he ordered. And just like, that they were dismissed from his podium.

Justice headed back to her seat with a confident strut knowing that, as usual, she had won the battle.

"The court will take a thirty-minute break and will resume right after." Judge Madison dismissed them so Clay could speak with his client.

As soon as court resumed, Clay gave the good news that his client had agreed to pay Naomi a full benefit package. He also agreed to change her status from fired to resignation.

"Thank you so much." Naomi gave Justice a hug.

"No problem; that's what I do," Justice smiled. "Stop by my office next week and we'll tie up the loose ends." Naomi walked away with a smile. Clearly she felt her victory.

"Justice, I have to give it to you. You drive a hard bargain in the courtroom. I knew you were going in for the kill sooner or later," Clay said, as he approached Justice's table to shake her hand.

"Council, as much as I enjoy your enthusiasm I wish we could have settled this yesterday . . . out of the courtroom. We have wasted months on the court's docket for something that could have been handled in one day."

"That may be true, but a fight with you is worth it." Clay gave Justice a flirtatious smile. "How about we grab some lunch?"

"Ah, Clayton . . ." Justice pretended to be disappointed, "I can't. Not today. I have plans. And I'm running behind schedule. I have to get going." Justice closed her briefcase rapidly and rushed off, escaping Clay. She rushed out into 90-degree boiling Mississippi heat and jumped into her fully loaded silver Mercedes-Benz CLS550 and sped off toward her aunt Mattie's house to grab some lunch. Clay had been trying to take her out on a date for the last couple of months, and she always turned him down with some excuse or another. He just wasn't her type. Clay was a good lawyer, but he was way too uptight for Justice. Justice didn't know how to tell him she wasn't interested. She just hoped that he would get the picture. Unfortunately, it was taking him longer than she would have liked. Maybe she could introduce him to someone else. She just didn't know who.

Justice finally pulled into Aunt Mattie's driveway behind Kiki's blue, four-door Ford Contour.

"Hey, baby," Aunt Mattie greeted Justice as soon as she walked into the living room.

"Hey, Auntie." Justice walked over and gave her a hug.

"I thought you weren't coming. Thought maybe you got held up in court."

"Almost. But I put an end to something that was trying to drag on." Justice set her keys and Coach bag down on the coffee table. Then she immediately sat and soaked up the comfort of her aunt's old cushion-pillowed sofa that she loved so much.

"Let me go ahead and fix ya a plate. I got some spaghetti, fried chicken, and corn bread. Just what you need to get your energy back, 'cause you look beat."

"Just a small portion, Auntie. If I eat too much I'll be too tired to work," Justice warned her, knowing how her aunt loved to fix healthy plates. Which was always way too much for Justice, especially when she was eating soul food. Diabetes and high blood pressure ran in her family, and she was trying her best to keep the odds down.

"What's up, Justice?" Kiki asked, coming down the hallway putting on some gold and pink hoop earrings.

"Nothing; just stopped by to grab some lunch."

"Umm. So you're eating lunch alone . . . again."

"No. I'm not eating lunch alone because both you and Aunt Mattie are here," Justice smiled.

"Well, I guess you can call us company," Kiki smiled back. "I can't stay though. I'm working the evening shift today. I'm covering for Deloris. She's out sick with the flu."

"Well, I'm only going to eat a bite because I need to get back to the office."

"Justice, baby, come on to the table. I got your plate ready," Aunt Mattie yelled from the dining area.

Justice got off the couch and headed toward the dining room with Kiki on her heels.

"I'm done with Quin," Kiki blurted out.

Justice wasn't shocked at all. Quin was like most guys that Kiki dated—unemployed or just plain losers. And most of the time they didn't even deny it. But Kiki thought she could bring out the good in them.

"What happened?" Justice inquired.

"Can you believe he quit his job because they asked him to work on Sundays? According, to him, he can't work on Sundays because he parties on Saturday nights. So he just quit. That was the last straw for me. I finally saw the light. He won't ever have anything. I'm done with guys like him. Besides, he had asked me for one too many rides. I told him he needs a job because he needs a car. I am not a cab."

Justice started laughing so hard she began coughing. Kiki could be funny like that sometimes. Justice just hoped she was serious about not dating guys like Quin any longer. She had tried to warn her cousin many times about those types of guys. But Kiki never listened. Justice secretly hoped it would be different next time around, but only time would tell because it never took Kiki long to move on to the next date.

Biting into her crispy fried chicken, Justice thought about that sexy guy she had bumped into at the courthouse in the hallway. Not only was he one of the sexiest guys she had seen in a long time, he looked like a pretty stand-up guy. Maybe Kiki could meet someone like him. But the picture in her head clearly showed her standing next to him and not Kiki. Shaking her head Justice quickly dismissed that scene right out of her mind. Besides, there was no chance she would ever even see that guy again.

ððð

The look Morgan had on her face two days before when Austin had dropped her off at swimming lessons had still been ripping his heart out, her telling him that she wouldn't go back home with her mom even if she did come back. He just couldn't understand how Monica could continue to hurt and disrupt their daughter's life. And although he was done giving her any more chances, he still had to figure out what to do to take action so that he could keep his daughter home with him for good. He was sitting at his desk flipping through a lineup book trying to put a profile together. However, his mind couldn't have been further from the pictures. His only thoughts concerned his daughter, and those thoughts were weighing heavy on him.

"What's going on with you, man?" Trent approached Austin's desk towering over him. Standing at 6 foot 7 inches tall, weighing 280 pounds, Trent was a force to be reckoned with. Trent had worked as a cop on the beat until he was injured in a domestic dispute gone bad. Now he worked as a homicide detective right along beside Austin. Working sixteen-hour shifts together sometimes, Trent knew Austin like the back of his hand. So he knew all too well when something was bothering him. And the way Austin was sitting at his desk looking straight through a lineup book clearly gave him up. Something was definitely wrong.

"Nothing. Just trying to get this lineup together." Austin flipped the book closed.

"Look, man, stop with the BS. What's on your mind? You've been acting strange for the last couple of days." Trent walked over and sat down at his desk which was right across from Austin's.

"Man, it's Monica. She ran off and left Morgan again."

"Not again!" Trent looked shocked.

"But this is the last time, though. I'm not letting her get away with it this time. Morgan's staying home with me. I can't keep letting her ruin Morgan's life."

"Have you heard from her since she left?"

"Not a word, man." Austin shook his head. "This time I'm taking legal action. I just got to figure out where to start or who to start with. I know I need a lawyer, of course, but who? I can't take any chances of anything being screwed up." Austin dropped his head in his hands and took a deep breath. They both sat in silence for two long minutes.

"Justice. That's who. Justice." Trent snapped two of his fingers together. He said, "She can help you, man. From what I hear, she's bad."

"Who is that? I mean, how she can help?" Austin asked with a confused looked on his face.

"She's a lawyer. And, man, she a ferocious one at that. Remember that airline company last year that won the case against their part-time employees? Remember? It was all over the newspapers and TV."

"Oh yeah. I heard about that." Austin sounded hopeful.

"Call her. Now."

"This is a different type of case, Trent. A little case, a nonexistent case compared to that one. She probably won't even take my call." Austin looked defeated.

"Look, man, it's worth a try. Plus, I hear good things about her taking all kinds of cases all the time. Lemme put it like this. Justice is your only hope."

In deep thought Austin picked up his pen and started to roll it around on his desk. He was thinking, what if Trent was right. What did he have to lose? It had to be at least worth a try. "Trent, would you happen to know her number?" Austin finally asked.

"I don't know the number, but the firm is called Rhem something. There's another name in the front of that. I think it starts with a G. Oh, it's called Garrett and Rhem law firm. Google it."

A stroke of a few keys and Austin had the number.

"Hi, I would like to speak with an attorney at your firm by the name of Justice." At that moment it occurred to him that he didn't even have her last name. But it must have been true what Trent said about her being "ferocious" because no last name was needed. The receptionist never asked.

He was immediately transferred to Tabitha, who identified herself as Justice's assistant. At first Tabitha seemed a little apprehensive about setting Austin up with a direct appointment with Justice, seeing that he only gave her the bare minimum information for his visit. So to smooth her over, he identified himself as a lead homicide detective who needed to discuss a very urgent matter with her. Clearly their office had respect for the badge because Tabitha set him up with an appointment right away. Austin hung up the phone feeling hopeful.

"I'm in."

"You got an appointment?"

"Yep, today. So, look, can you pick Morgan up from school and drop her off at the YMCA for her swimming lesson?"

"Absolutely. You just go handle your business," Trent reassured him.

With that, Austin grabbed his keys and bolted for the parking lot. If this meeting went well his worries could soon be over.

Chapter Three

Glad to be back at her office and out of that hot Mississippi heat, Justice quickly but carefully unsnapped the buttons on the jacket of her Nanette Lepore designer skirt suit. After all the years she had been living in Mississippi the one thing she just couldn't seem to get used to was the heat. The only thing she did like about the heat was the tan she would get on hot days like the one she was experiencing. Growing up in Mississippi had not always been easy for her. The color of her skin always got her strange looks from both races because not only was she black, she was mixed with Latino. Both blacks and whites always assumed she was mixed with white blood. So she was either too white for the blacks or too black for the whites. And after she entered high school, she had grown tired and given up explaining her color to anyone. She was just Justice, a girl from the Big Apple who couldn't understand why her skin tone, curly hair, and green eyes were such a big deal to everyone else. But on hot days when the sun would beam 100 degrees, she could get that skin tone that she always craved, a hint of buttercream with a splash of mocha chocolate.

Knock, knock.

Saundra

Tabitha lightly tapped on Justice's office door which was ajar. "Here's your after-lunch latte." She strolled in set the Starbucks cup down on Justice's desk.

Tabitha always made a special stop by Starbucks on her way back from lunch to grab Justice a latte. Justice used to protest, explaining that it wasn't part of her job description, but Tabitha refused to hear any of it. Justice had been good to her. When she had first started at the firm Tabitha had been going through a rough divorce. She would have to leave work during the day, but Justice had hung in there with her until she got through it. And she had appreciated that. Not too many bosses would understand that sometimes life had rough patches that you had to plow through and get over. So it was Tabitha's pleasure to grab Justice a latte after lunch daily. No, she didn't mind, not one bit. Justice had a good heart, and Tabitha knew it was only a matter of time before God put someone in her life that she could share that good heart with.

"Thank you, Tabitha." Justice hung her jacket up to ensure it stay wrinkle free.

Tabitha sat down in a chair facing Justice's desk to brief her on all her messages while she was out. "OK, most of your day is still free. Candice stepped out for a bit, but she completed the Jackson vs. Hardnabrigg and Associates deposition. The full deposition has been e-mailed to you and here is the hard copy of it on a disk." Tabitha handed Justice the disk. "Mr. Rhem called. He wants you to schedule an appointment with your associates first thing in the morning. He will be bringing in Willis from Empowerment to discuss the new account."

"Wait, I have that thing in the morning," Justice cut in.

"Not to worry. I have already set up the appointment with the associates, and I cleared your calendar."

Justice smiled inside. Tabitha was a wonderful assistant, and she knew that when she hired her she had made the right decision. Tabitha had been going through a lot when she first got the job, but she had been honest with Justice from day one. And she had never let her personnel life affect her work responsibilities, and Justice respected her for that. Sure, she had to leave work at odd times during the day back then, but her work was always prompt and on time. And Justice never missed a message or deadline.

"That's pretty much it. But you do have one last appointment that should be here any minute."

"Any minute?" Justice had a look of concern on her face. She didn't have anything set up at this time for today. And she hardly ever took unexpected appointments.

"There is a Detective Crews who called and needed to speak with you right away."

"Detective Crews?" Justice repeated the name out loud. But it still didn't ring a bell. "Regarding what?"

"He really wouldn't give any information."

"Tabitha, you know I don't take appointments this way."

"I know, but he said it was urgent. And the sound of his voice was urgent. Either way, he should be here soon." Tabitha stood up. "Can I get you anything else?"

"No, just let me know when this Detective Crews gets here," Justice said in a sort of an exaggerated tone.

"OK." Tabitha smiled as she left the office.

Justice picked up her latte and took a sip. She needed the energy to stay awake. That soul food she had devoured at her aunt Mattie's house was having an effect. While sipping on her latte she pondered over this detective. She didn't have any clients who were in jail or on their way to jail. So she was clearly puzzled. Suddenly, her phone started to buzz so she picked it up.

"Detective Crews is here," Tabitha chimed on the other end of the phone. From the sound of Tabitha's voice, Justice knew he must have been fine, because anytime Justice had a good-looking client, Tabitha all but sang into the phone.

"Bring him in." Justice sat up in her chair and awaited her client in a professional manner as she always did.

The door slowly swung open and behind Tabitha stood one of the sexiest men Gulfport, Mississippi, had to offer. And Justice remembered him right away. It was the guy she had almost knocked over at the courthouse. She quickly gathered her composure that was threatening to fall apart.

"Detective, have a seat." Justice motioned toward a chair.

Austin made his way to one of the plush chairs that sat directly in front of Justice's desk. But just barely. He almost went weak at the knees when he noticed the beautiful woman sitting behind the desk. He remembered her right away. There was no mistaking her. He hadn't seen a woman as beautiful as her in many years. And his heart wouldn't push away the feelings that he had felt the first time he saw her. He was hopelessly in love. He was sure it was written across his face and ready to be proclaimed from his lips. Instead, he said, "We have met before. Remember, we ran into each other down at the courthouse a couple of days ago."

"Oh yeah. Again, I'm sorry." Justice apologized again trying to appear normal and not smitten by his natural good looks. The guy was a masterpiece.

Austin smiled. "Again, it's OK." He couldn't stop staring into her beautiful green eyes. He had to gather himself together. He had forgotten why he was there.

"You needed to speak to me, Detective?" Justice broke his trance.

"Ah yes. Well, it's about my daughter. I need to get full custody of her. And, well, I was told that you were the best. And quite frankly, I need the best."

Justice was a little taken aback. Here she was thinking he needed to see her about something serious. And all he wanted was custody of his daughter. What type of lawyer did he think she was? Or maybe this was a joke? But he wasn't laughing. He looked serious.

"Mr. Crews, I'm not sure who referred you to me, but I handle high-profile cases. I sometimes take on small cases but only by request. Now I can have my assistant refer you to some—" Austin cut her off.

"Look, I know that this is small fries to you. But I don't want anybody else to handle this. My daughter is twelve years old. She is my life, and she needs me right now. You are the only chance I have at making things right for her."

"Mr. Crews, my heart goes out to you and your daughter."

"Morgan."

"Excuse me?" Justice inquired.

"Her name is Morgan. My daughter's name is Morgan. Now maybe you misunderstood what I just said." Austin kept a serious but respectful tone although a single tear threatened to roll down his cheek. "Morgan has been through a lot of disappointments in her life. And now she needs me. I do not want to disappoint her. So I need you to help me, and I can assure you that money is not an object. Maybe you could think about it for a couple of days. I will leave my contact information up front with your assistant. Thanks for your time, Justice. I know you are busy." Austin gave a slight smile as he stood up and turned to leave. He felt she had dismissed him before hearing what he had to say.

"Mr. Crews."

Austin stopped in his tracks and turned around to face her.

"I'll do it. I'll take the case," Justice released.

"You'll take it?" Austin couldn't believe his ears.

"Yes, but you have to be available to consult. I know you detectives live very unpredictable lives. But this firm is busy. We don't have time to chase anyone."

"Don't worry. When you call I will answer."

"As long as we are clear." Justice used her hard edge so he would know the severity of what she had said. "Leave all your information with Tabitha, and we'll be in touch soon."

"I really appreciate this." Austin gave her one last glance before he opened the door and hurriedly left before she had a change of heart.

Justice didn't know what made her change her mind. Maybe it was the mention of his daughter needing her father. She had always had a sense of needing her own father, but the pure fact was, she had never met him. He had died before she was born in a train accident. And the look the detective had on his face when he said his daughter needed him broke protected barriers in her heart. A slight rap on her door broke her thoughts.

"Come in, Tabitha." Justice knew it had to be her.

"You took his case?" Tabitha all but jumped on Justice's desk and did a dance.

"How did you know he had a case?" Justice asked.

"He told me," Tabitha smiled.

"I guess he don't waste valuable time." Justice sipped her latte again.

"I guess not." Tabitha continued to grin. "But you should definitely let him take you out. He looks good. Not only that, he's interested in you. You should have seen the smile on his face when he came out of here."

"Tabitha, he is not interested in me. He is just happy I took his case. Besides, I don't date my clients. Remember?" Justice kept a straight face.

"I remember," Tabitha nodded. "But *that's* going to be your husband," she predicted and abruptly closed the door as she quickly exited the office.

Chapter Four

Justice pulled her car into the parking lot of Shady Grove Park. She absolutely loved to run at this park. It had a nice trail full of trees, it was peaceful, and she could run freely without being stopped by cars. Shady Grove ran a full circle around the downtown area. It was the biggest park in Gulfport. Many people visited the park every day to run, walk, or just have a seat on the many benches scattered throughout the area. She always met up with Kiki on Saturday and Sunday mornings to do a six-mile run.

Kiki pulled in just as Justice climbed out of her car. Kiki quickly parked and got out.

"Good morning, Justice. You beat me here this morning. I'm shocked. Normally, I run around the whole park before you decide to even show up," Kiki joked.

"Well, I'm proud to announce that I got a good night's sleep. I actually went to bed without a migraine. Can you believe it?" Justice beamed feeling refreshed. She started to do her prestretches before the run.

"Ummm, no headache? That's odd, but good. Wait a minute! Is there some guy you ain't tellin' me about?" Kiki threw her hand on her right hip. "'Cause you know I don't like being in the dark."

"There is no guy." Justice let out a slight laugh. "Kiki, you are so weird. You always think it's a guy. Can't a girl just feel good sometimes?"

"Humph," Kiki sighed, giving her the benefit of the doubt. "I hope one day it is about a guy. You don't need to be alone. Some male company would do you good."

"No, running these six miles will do me good. Now, let's go." Justice took off, and Kiki followed.

"Hey, slow down! I'm not trying to hurt none of this size six. I have to take very good care of it. And running at this speed I could easily break a limb," Kiki babbled for fun.

"All right, I guess I could slow down to our usual speed," Justice chirped while falling into step of their normal running speed.

"So what have you been up to this week? I haven't heard much from you. You've called my phone all of twice this week," Justice asked.

"I thought I would give you a break," Kiki smiled. "But actually, I've been working a lot of extra hours for Deloris."

"She's still out?"

"Yep. Turns out she's going to have that flu for seven more months."

"Wait a minute. She's pregnant?"

"Yep."

"I thought she got her tubes tied after the last one."

"Turns out she missed the appointment and never rescheduled it."

"Wow. So that makes baby number . . .?"

"Six. And she is *still* not married," Kiki told her. "And this one seems to be giving her the blues. She can't seem to keep anything down, and her blood pressure is through the roof. So the doctor put her on bed rest."

"Well, to you, I say, enjoy the hours," Justice smiled.

"I guess, since I don't have a love life right now."

"Is Quin still out?" Justice inquired, hoping she'd get the answer she was looking for.

"Yep."

Justice smiled feeling relieved.

"But he was trying to call. I told him the only way we would get back together was if the Jackson Five did. So he stopped calling." Kiki started laughing.

"You crazy, Kiki," Justice laughed.

"But I have another man report. I'm walking in the Piggly Wiggly the other day, and this guy walks up to me lookin' so fine. He had that goatee thing going on, and I really like that. So he asks me out on a date, and I had to say yes."

"So now you are meeting guys in the grocery store?" Just when Justice thought she was improving.

"It's not like that, Justice. He walked over, introduced himself, and he sounded like a good guy. So I said, why not? Plus, his name is not ghetto. It may be a good sign."

"What's his name?" Justice asked.

"Robert," Kiki blushed.

Justice stopped in her tracks. Then she burst into laughter. "Kiki, I don't know if you will ever change."

"What?" Kiki stopped running to join Justice.

"Nothing. So when is the date?" Justice pushed a strand of hair from her face.

"Tonight."

"Well, good luck. Now let's get finished with this run so we can grab some fresh fruit and yogurt," Justice finalized.

ððð

Austin and Morgan pulled into County Market shopping center. Morgan looked around the parking lot noticing all the cars. That's when she, without a doubt, knew this wouldn't be an in-and-out run. They only needed to grab a few things for breakfast, but looking around the parking lot Morgan was sure they would be in there until lunch.

"Dad, there are way too many cars out here I just hope all these people are not inside the store," Morgan babbled as they climbed out of the truck. Since it was the weekend they were in Austin's 2010 fully loaded all-black Cadillac Escalade instead of the squad car.

"I don't know, sweetheart, but we only need to grab a couple of things, and were out of here," Austin confirmed as the automatic doors opened and they entered the store. And Morgan's fears were confirmed. The store was packed. It was Saturday morning, and everyone was out doing their weekend shopping. Morgan grabbed a shopping cart and fell into step with her dad.

"So, Dad, when do you think I will get to see Grandma Tess again? I haven't seen her in like three years. I miss her so much, Dad." Grandma Tess was Austin's mom. She hadn't flown out to Gulfport in the last three years. Since she retired, she spent a lot of time volunteering, and it was hard to get her to leave New York, which was Austin's hometown.

"I don't know, sweetheart. I've been thinking about that too. As soon as I take care of some things here and get some downtime, we can look into taking a flight out. In the meantime, we just have to keep calling her on the phone."

"I know. It's just not the same as when we see her in person." Morgan appeared sad.

"Speaking of going to New York, what would think about moving there?" Austin reached for a box of Instant Quaker Grits.

"You mean living there? Why would we do that?"

Austin turned toward the fruit and vegetable section. "There's a chance in the future that my job may transfer there, but it's not definite yet. But I just would like to know how you feel about that transition. I know you have never lived anywhere else and all of your friends are here. It would be a huge change." Austin reached to pick up some bananas.

"You know what, Dad? I wouldn't mind because I would be close to Grandma Tess and I would be with you. I could always make . . ." Morgan's voice seemed to trail off as Austin looked off to the right of him and saw who he believed to be Justice standing there. She was picking up peaches and testing them in her hand with a huge grin on her face. Talk about a Colgate smile, hers was perfect.

Morgan noticed that her dad wasn't listening to her anymore because he seemed to be staring at some lady not too far from them. And for a moment Morgan thought she saw her dad smile. Before she could ask him any questions, he had turned to the unknown lady.

"Hi, Justice."

Justice was totally caught off guard. There was Austin facing her. Suddenly she felt embarrassed. Here she was in her workout gear. She looked a mess, but she didn't know why she was concerned about the way she looked. "Hi, Austin." Then they both just stood there for a moment.

"This is my daughter, Morgan." Austin pointed to a girl behind him that looked exactly like him. She had her hair pulled back in a ponytail, and it really showed off her high cheekbones, not to mention she was already about 5 foot 6 and at age twelve, she was bound to get taller. Justice couldn't help but notice that in a few years she would be ready for the runway. She was strikingly beautiful.

"Hi, Morgan." Justice extended her hand.

"Hi," Morgan said quickly, then she turned her attention back to Austin.

Kiki nudged Justice's shoulder to get her attention. Justice had completely forgotten she was there. "Oh, this is my cousin, Kiki." Justice slightly pulled Kiki forward.

"Hi," Austin spoke to Kiki.

"Hey," Kiki spoke with a huge grin covering her face.

"Kiki and I just finished our early-morning run, so we just stopped in to grab some breakfast," Justice said, and waved the peach in front of her. She didn't know why she felt the need to explain. Austin seemed to make her forget herself. And a peach hardly passed as breakfast. She was sure he thought she was some weird health-craved attorney.

"Morgan and I also needed to grab some breakfast," Austin said. Silence again.

"Well, I'll being seeing you." Austin ended the silence. "And it was nice meeting you, Kiki."

"You too." Kiki still grinned from ear to ear.

With that being said, Austin and Morgan headed toward the counter. Once out of sight, Morgan stopped pushing the shopping cart. "How do you know that lady, Dad?"

"She's a lawyer. I've been meaning to discuss some other things with you. But let's get out of here first." Austin couldn't get his mind off Justice. He absolutely loved the way she looked in her workout gear. Not that she needed to work out. Her body was great. She had all the right curves, but he had to get a hold of himself. Now she was his lawyer, and he was her client. He had to keep it professional, even though he didn't have a clue as to how. He had fallen for someone he barely even knew. She probably didn't even know he existed. She was out of his league. But there was something almost familiar about her, like the way she talked. Being from New York, he had a Northern accent versus that Southern drawl that Mississippians possessed. However, Justice didn't have that drawl. When she spoke, there was just something about her that was definitely familiar to him.

"OK, Justice, who was that?" Kiki struggled to keep up with her cousin. As soon as they were out of Austin's sight, Justice had increased her speed.

"A new client," she replied without looking at Kiki.

"Is he married?"

"Why?" Justice stopped in front of the yogurt.

"'Cause he is fine, that's why. And you need a man ASAP."

"Kiki, didn't you just hear what I said? He's my client. And I don't date my clients." Justice reached for her favorite yogurt, strawberry.

"Is that some type of work ethics or something?" Kiki asked sarcastically.

"Yes, it happens to be for me. Now here." Justice passed Kiki her favorite yogurt, peach. Then Justice started toward the checkout counter.

"Ummm." Kiki sucked her teeth. "I'm glad I'm not a lawyer. And anyway, maybe you should drop him as a client because he is sweet on you. I could tell by the way he spoke to you."

Justice stopped in her tracks and faced Kiki. "Look, that man is not interested in me. Just because someone speaks to you does not mean they are about to propose. Now, can we please drop it and get out of here?"

"All right. You don't have to be so testy." Kiki smiled and fell into step with Justice toward the checkout counter.

Chapter Five

"Tabitha, can you bring me in a bottle of water? Thanks," Justice said through the phone. She was sitting at her desk with a light migraine coming on. She thought it best she take something before it progressed into a huge one. She had just left court for the morning, and now she was preparing paperwork she would need for the day.

"Here you go." Tabitha passed her the cold Aqua water bottle.

"Thanks," Justice said, as she popped the pills into her mouth.

"Are you going to be OK?" Tabitha look concerned.

"Yeah, I'll be fine. It hasn't come on strong so I'm just trying to stop it before it gets there. This will knock it right out," Justice said, referring to the two Extra Strength Excedrin pills she had just swallowed. "Can you make a couple of copies of these? Mr. Crews should be here any moment to sign them."

"Right away." Tabitha reached for the papers. "After he gets here, I'll be taking off to lunch. Your calendar is clear until 3:00 P.M. Then you have that meeting with Mr. Grafftin on the fourth floor in conference room B. What would like for lunch? I'll pick it for you."

"Oh, Tabitha, you are a lifesaver. I'll have some Chinese. You already know what I like."

"OK, I'll give you buzz when Mr. Crews arrives." Tabitha exited the office with certainty.

Justice decided to check her e-mails before Austin arrived. As she read them she noticed that her headache was gone just as quickly as it had tried to invade.

Tabitha slightly knocked on the door before entering. She approached the desk with the copies in her hand. "Here you go, all stapled and ready to sign. And Mr. Crews has arrived. I'll give you a moment, and then send him in." Tabitha smiled and laid the copies on her desk.

"Tabitha, why are you smiling?" Justice questioned.

"No reason."

"Go ahead and send in Mr. Crews and you can take off to lunch." Justice smiled back and dismissed Tabitha with a friendly wave.

"Good morning, Mr. Crews." Justice stood up and extended her hand for a handshake when he entered the office.

"Good morning, and please call me Austin."

"Mr. Crews, you are my client, so it is only professional that I address you by your last name."

"No, please, I insist. Call me Austin." He smiled so hard Justice felt her eyes flutter.

"If you insist . . . Austin." Justice smiled and gestured her hands in a sitting motion for Austin to have a seat.

"And if you don't mind my asking, what is your last name? I mean, I haven't seen it anywhere in your office or on your door. It just says Justice. Surely you have a last name."

"Yes, I have a last name. It's Lopez. I just never use it. Everyone calls me Justice. It's the only name I will answer to."

"Good, because I happen to think it's an awesome name. I wouldn't want to call you anything else."

Either he was openly flittering with her or being very modest. She was not exactly sure which, but she had to gain control of the situation. He was here on business, and they should get right down to it. Besides, she was in no way flattered; at least that's what she had convinced herself.

"OK, Mr. Crews, I mean, Austin," Justice corrected herself. "I have these papers for you to sign," she said as she reached for the documents Tabitha had just put on her desk. "I went before the judge this morning on your behalf and got temporary custody of Morgan. So she is legally in your custody until we go back to court."

"Just like that? You just went before the judge, and he gave me temporary custody without me being there? You are good," Austin complimented her with a smile.

"Well, you made it very clear when you were in my office last week that this was an urgent matter that needed to be dealt with. It's really not rocket science; the other parent is absent, and you are present."

"Wow, thanks," was all Austin could say. He was really impressed and elated that the process was moving in a positive direction. "So what do we do next? I mean, when will we have to go to court for the actual custody?"

"Well, the judge gave me a sixty-day continuance, but I am trying to push it through faster. I see no need to drag our feet. Tabitha will get the court dates set and approved. My paralegal Candice will check some things out on Monica, the absent parent, and we will proceed. I will let you know what the date will be, but it should be set in the next 30 days."

"I'll be ready."

"Another thing. I will have to meet with you and Morgan to go over some things. I will need to talk with Morgan and ask her some questions. I have to make sure she is prepared when we go to court."

"Wait a minute. Morgan has to go to court?" Austin's look changed from happy to concern.

"Absolutely. The judge likes to speak with the child and get his or her insight on the situation. The judge wants to be sure the child is aware of what's going on. A lot of times it weighs heavy on his ultimate decision. I hope this is not going to be a problem." Justice noticed his concerned look. She also saw maybe even a little hesitation.

"Uh, no, it will be fine. I just didn't know she would have to go to court. I mean, she knows what's going on. I just will have to explain the court thing to her."

"All right, fine. I will give you a couple of days to work on that before we have our first meeting together. We will have to meet a least three times before we actually go to court. I have to make sure she is really prepared. It also gives you time if you were to have a change of heart should the mother return."

"I won't be having a change of heart, you can trust me on that. Let's get things on the road for Morgan's sake. She has been through enough." Austin scooted to the edge of his chair. "Now, where do I sign?"

"Right here." Justice pushed the papers in his direction. "I will have Tabitha call with the date of our first meeting. Will mornings or evenings work better for you?" she questioned.

"Evenings work for me. But you are not planning to have them here, are you?"

"Not exactly in my office, but we would be here at the firm. We will have time scheduled in one of our conference rooms." She could tell by the look on his face that he had something else in mind.

"I know this may not be normal, but I was thinking maybe you could come to my house." The look on Justice's face went from professional lawyer to you must be crazy, so he had to explain. "Wait a minute. Let me explain my reasoning. I wouldn't want to bring Morgan here; I just think she would feel more comfortable talking to you if she was at home in her own environment." Austin presented his reason.

"Look, Mr. Cre . . . Austin, you are right. I don't normally meet with my clients at their homes. It's just not . . . well, you know . . . professional."

"I totally understand, but it would mean a lot to Morgan. And I promise it won't be strictly business. I'll even cook." Austin gave her a slight smile.

"I just don't know," she protested.

"Please."

"All right, OK. But just this once. After this meeting Morgan should be comfortable and I will explain to her we have to meet here." Justice meant what she had just said.

"Thanks, Justice. You won't be sorry. Oh, and I brought my checkbook with me today. How much is the fee? What should I make it out for?" Austin pulled out his checkbook prepared to write.

"It isn't going to cost you anything," Justice said matter-of-factly.

"What do you mean it's not going to cost me? You are an attorney, aren't you?"

"Of course, I am an attorney." Justice was caught off guard.

"Then surely there is a fee involved. Now, you just tell me how much, and I'll write you a check."

"Austin, every year I take a case or so that's not high profile, and I do them pro bono. I usually take high-profile cases. Those cases cost a lot of money. A case like this at this firm would only cost between ten to fifteen thousand dollars, which is considered low profile, so on occasion when I take a low-profile case I do it pro bono. Trust me, it's OK. This is the most prestigious firm in the entire state of Mississippi. We make millions. We take clients from all over. I assure you, we can afford it."

"And I appreciate the gesture, really I do. But I can afford this; I may only be a homicide detective, but trust me, I am well reserved. Paying for this is not a problem. Now, you said ten to fifteen thousand. How about I just make it fifteen thousand?" Austin started writing without another word.

Justice knew he was being stubborn. She knew stubbornness when she saw it because sometimes she could be the same way. Her auntie Mattie told her so all the time. She stood up. "Austin, stop writing. Now you can write the check, but this firm will not accept it." Justice gave him a look that told him that was it. It would be her way or the highway. Austin immediately realized he liked her take-charge mentality. Maybe that's the way she was in court. Whatever it was, he got the point so he dropped the pen and didn't protest any further.

"Like I said, I will cook dinner, and we will meet at my house. Does Friday around 6:00 work for you?" Austin asked.

"I think that should be fine," Justice agreed.

Austin immediately wrote his address on the back of one of his detective cards and passed it to her. "We'll see you Friday." He left her office feeling he had accomplished something. She was definitely a take-charge woman, and he liked that. And Friday was too far away.

Justice didn't know what she had just committed herself to—having a meeting at her client's house, the same client that Kiki and Tabitha told her was interested in her. But it wasn't about him. It was for his daughter, Morgan. And Morgan was an important part of the case. Her well-being was at stake. Justice couldn't possibly deny that. It was business only. No strings attached. Strictly a client-and-attorney meeting. There was nothing wrong with that. Besides, it wouldn't happen again. Just this one time.

Chapter Six

"Come on, Morgan, push it, push it; you can do it," Coach Davis urged her on. "You're almost done. Stay afloat and stretch." Morgan was swimming like her life depended on it. Austin sat in the stands by the pool amazed at how far his daughter had come. Just a few short weeks ago she could barely float in the water. Now here she was swimming a whole lap to show her strength in the water. He was really proud. Cynthia Davis, her coach, had promised him that she would take good care of her and make her a quality swimmer, and from the looks of it, she was well on her way.

"Good job," Austin clapped as Morgan reached the end her of last lap. Balancing herself by holding on to the edge of the pool Morgan looked in Austin's direction and gave him a huge grin.

"Mr. Crews," Coach Davis said, with her hand extended, "Morgan is really improving. I think she may have some of that professional swimming blood in her. It's not often that I have such a strong swimmer in this short turnaround. I mean, she is racing with some of our prize swimmers."

"I knew I could trust you to get her where I wanted her to be, and that's just a safe swimmer. But I don't think she is interested in competing. I mean, she hasn't said anything to me." Austin gave a nod in Morgan's direction as she headed toward him.

"Well, maybe she isn't, but she is really good. I just thought you should know," Coach Davis implied before walking toward another parent.

"Thanks, Coach Davis, I'll keep that in mind." Austin watched as Morgan approached. It didn't surprise him one bit that Morgan's swimming was turning out so unique. Monica had been a prize swimmer, so it was definitely in her blood.

"Hey, Dad," Morgan said, smiling.

"Hey, Pumpkin."

"Dad," Morgan looked around to make sure no one heard her, "somebody might hear. You keep forgetting I'm twelve now. 'Pumpkin' is too immature," she whispered while looking over her shoulder to make sure the coast was still clear.

"Sorry, sweetheart," Austin smiled. "So do you want to go for burgers?"

"Sure, I'll be right back." Morgan skipped off toward the locker room. Austin stood back and admired some of the other swimmers. He admired how good some of them were and wondered if they would go pro one day.

ᗄᗄᗄ

Straight to Sam's Juicy Burgers is where they headed when they left the YMCA.

"Dad, I'm so glad you decided to come here. I need all the grease I can get after that practice." Morgan flipped her menu open, already knowing what she wanted.

"I see your swimming has improved substantially." Austin complimented as the waitress approached. They placed their orders without any hesitation. They both loved the burgers at Sam's Juicy Burgers, so they never needed extra time to look at the menu.

"Yeah, Coach thinks I'm doing great."

"She told me. She seems to think you have pro blood."

"No, Dad, I'm really not that good." Morgan smiled and took a sip of her double strawberry milk shake that the waitress had just delivered.

"Yeah, you are. Have you thought about training to compete?"

Morgan looked up from her milk shake with a sort of sadness. "Compete? No, Dad, this was just so I could learn to swim, remember? I am not Mom; swimming is not what I want to do." Morgan took her concentration back to her milk shake. Austin knew she wouldn't want to compete because of Monica. Competing would make her think of Monica. And Morgan seemed hard set against memories of her mother. She was upset, but Austin knew that time would make it better. And he would give her that.

"I understand, OK?" Austin soothed the conversation. "I just want you to know that if that's what you want to do I will support you."

"I know. And now I am just enjoying learning the sport," Morgan smiled.

Austin thought this would be a good time to talk with her about Justice and the whole custody situation. He had to prepare her for Justice's visit. The waitress approached the table with their orders.

"Do you need anything else?" the waitress asked, as she prepared to leave the table.

Austin looked at Morgan to see if she needed anything, and Morgan shook her head and smiled, and then turned her focus toward the ketchup for her fries.

"You remember, Justice, right?" Austin asked.

"Who?" Morgan asked, knowing exactly who Justice was.

"Remember, I introduced you to her at the supermarket, and I told you in the car that I had spoken with her about helping me get custody of you."

"Yeah, I remember." Morgan took the first bite out of her hamburger.

"Well, she is taking the case. The judge has already granted temporary custody to me because of her." Austin grinned, but he wondered why he didn't get the same reaction from Morgan. "Does that make you happy? It means you are with me no matter what until we take this to court."

"Yes, Dad, I'm happy," Morgan said, half smiling. "I'm just shocked that she did it that fast." She had no idea her dad had spoken with Justice again. She remembered the look her dad had in his eyes when he saw Justice at the store. Something about him was different; he didn't see Justice like all the other women she had seen him speak to when they were out in public.

"Well, the next thing will be court, and you have to be a part of this. So Justice has to speak with you."

"Speak with me? Why, Dad?" Morgan questioned.

"She has to be sure you understand what's taking place, Morgan. The judge may want to ask you questions."

Morgan sat still for a moment with a blank look on her face that Austin couldn't read. "Sweetheart, trust me, this is all for the best. You do trust me, don't you?"

"Yes, Daddy. You know I trust you," Morgan assured him.

"OK. And don't worry, I'll be right there with you the whole time." Morgan nodded her head OK before taking another bite of her hamburger. Austin followed suit, taking a huge bit out of his burger.

"Umm, this is good," he complimented with a mouth full of burger.

"So, Dad, when will I speak with Justice?" Morgan asked.

"This Friday. I invited her over for dinner."

"You invited her to our house?" Morgan was again shocked.

"Yeah, I figured it would be a better atmosphere for you. Don't worry, it'll be fine." Austin popped fries into his mouth. Looking at her father relish his food Morgan decided to do the same.

Chapter Seven

Following the directions on her GPS system Justice navigated easily through the stop signs and left and right turns until she finally saw 1981 Bay Drive. Almost passing the house she backed up a little and pulled into the driveway next to Austin's squad car. She sat for a brief moment and took in the scenery; the neighbor was beautiful and quiet. Austin's home looked lovely from the outside. It was a brick ranch-style house with a two-car garage. A little nervous but not really sure why, Justice climbed out of the car and opened the door to the backseat. She reached in and retrieved her briefcase.

Finally making her way up the walkway to the door Justice rang the doorbell without further hesitation. The door swung open so abruptly she thought someone must have been standing behind it waiting.

"Hi, Morgan." Justice spoke first, noticing her right away. Justice extended her hand for a shake.

"Hi," Morgan replied back, gloomily ignoring her hand. "Dad," she turned and yelled.

Austin appeared right away with a welcoming smile on his face. "Justice," he spoke. "Come on in. I thought I heard the bell ring. I was out back grabbing the last of the wings off the grill. Come on in," he repeated since Justice seemed reluctant to move. She stepped in past Morgan and Austin.

Austin led the way to the den through the living room where the kitchen opened up. And off to the left of the kitchen was a clear view of the backyard that contained an in-ground swimming pool. It was absolutely beautiful. One thing Justice knew for sure. It was definitely a bachelor's pad, but Austin had some mad decorating skills. The den contained a Tosh brown sectional sofa with solid fabric colors and stripes. And just like any bachelor's pad, there was a 46-inch flat-screen TV on the wall. She was sure he sat there and consumed all of his sports. "You have a lovely home," she complimented.

"Thank you," Austin smiled. "Have a seat anywhere on the sofa. Can I get you something to drink?"

"Water would be fine." Justice took a seat. As she watched Austin go into the kitchen she noticed he was dressed casual for the first since she met him. He had on a pair of khaki polo shorts and a baby blue Polo shirt with a pair of fresh white Forces. Justice thought he looked deliciously handsome.

Morgan seemed to have disappeared somewhere between the living room and the den. Justice thought only momentarily about the greeting they had shared at the door. She wondered if Morgan had purposely not shaken her hand or if she had not seen it. But she decided to dismiss it. She wanted to get down to the business at hand.

"Here you go. I hope you like Dasani," Austin said, referring to the bottled water.

"Yes, Dasani is fine. So have you had time to discuss things with Morgan?"

"I explained to her about you coming over and how important this whole situation was. So I think everything should go well today. Feel free to ask her whatever you need to."

It wasn't until then that Justice noticed that Austin didn't have that Southern drawl that she was so used to hearing when speaking with someone from the South. But she decided not to pry at this point as to where he was from. She knew it would eventually come up, but she knew one thing was certain. He, like her, was far from home.

"Well, Morgan has set the table for dinner. I just need to grab a few things out of the kitchen. Dinner will be at the dining table in the room off to your right. I figured you can ask Morgan any questions you may have during dinner. I hope that's OK."

"That's fine," Justice replied.

"I'll get Morgan out here for dinner. I have hand soap by the kitchen sink so you can wash your hands," Austin said, then headed off to locate Morgan.

Justice got off the couch and went into the kitchen where she admired all of the stainless steel appliances just as she had furnished throughout her kitchen. She also took notice of the hardwood floors that seemed to run through the house. Not a scuff in sight, and they glowed with the perfect shine. After washing her hands, she scrolled off toward the table where Austin and Morgan had already taken their seats.

"Go ahead and have a seat anywhere you would like," Austin said, sitting at the head of the table.

Justice decided to sit across from Morgan since most of her conversation would be directed toward her. She also took notice of the food that had been placed on the table. It was a feast. There was garden salad, lasagna, chicken wings, and hot buttered rolls. It was at that moment she realized she had missed lunch. Her day had been one meeting after the other at the office and she just couldn't get away. But she would portion herself. She didn't want them to think she was a pig.

"I hope you are hungry," Austin said.

"Everything looks delicious. Did you prepare everything?"

"All but the salad. Morgan did that." Austin smiled in Morgan's direction. Morgan smiled back at her dad but fail to give Justice any eye contact.

"Well, the salad looks delicious too." Justice complimented.

As they started to fix their plates Justice decided to break the ice with Morgan who seemed withdrawn. "So, Morgan, what school do you attend?"

"Bay View Middle," Morgan replied, and quickly filled her mouth with lasagna.

"What grade are you?"

"Seventh." Again Morgan answered the question and hurried back to her food.

"Wow, seventh grade is like a new start coming from grade school." Justice tried to continue the conversation.

"Yeah, I remember those years for me. Grade school was the best. It was life on easy street," Austin joked.

"For me too. I really enjoyed it." Justice took a bite of her roll. "Do you enjoy living in Gulfport?"

"Of course I enjoy living here. It's the only place I have ever lived on earth," Morgan replied. Justice couldn't help but notice the annoyance in her tone. But she decided to continue on with the questions.

"How do you like living in this beautiful home with your dad?" Justice smiled.

"What do you mean? I love living with my dad," Morgan replied with her mouth full of lasagna.

"Morgan, don't talk with your mouth full." Austin gave her a stern look.

"Sorry, Dad."

Justice smiled. "It's OK, Austin. I mean, I guess I am asking her questions while she is eating her dinner. I totally understand." Justice got quiet for a couple of minutes while they continued to eat.

"So, Morgan, how would you feel about living with your dad permanently?"

Morgan looked up from her plate and looked directly at Justice. She took a big swig from her glass of water. "Dad, can I be excused?"

"No. Justice came here to speak with you. And now you are being rude."

"Austin, it's OK. We can do this another time. Thank you, Morgan, for talking with me."

"Now can I please be excused?" Morgan asked again.

"Yes," Austin said, clearly shocked with his daughter's behavior. Morgan marched off toward her room, clearly not happy.

"I am so sorry," Austin apologized. "I have never seen her behave that way. But she has been going through it. And she really misses Monica."

"It's really not a problem. We can try again. Sometimes children are just uncomfortable with this situation. But we'll work it out."

"Thank you so much, Justice, for understanding. It really means a lot to me."

"Again, it's not a problem." Justice took a sip of her water and gently set the glass back on the table. "I guess I'll get going." She started to scramble out of her chair.

"No, you don't have to leave. Finish your plate. Do you want more?"

"Ah, no, I'm fine. I had enough, and it was delicious."

"Are you sure? I can fix you up a plate to go," Austin offered.

"Thanks but no thanks. I'm stuffed," Justice lied. She was nowhere near stuffed as hungry as she was. She could have eaten a pig. But she was a lady. There was no way she would let him know that when she missed a meal she could have a hefty appetite. She would just go home, devour some fruit, jump in the shower, and she would be fine.

"OK, let me grab your briefcase, and I'll walk you out." Austin headed in the den to grab her briefcase. He was back within seconds, and they walked outside to her car.

"I want to thank you again for coming over to talk with Morgan. I know you didn't have to do that. And I really appreciate it."

"No problem. You're my client, and I want you and Morgan to feel comfortable during this transition," Justice assured him.

"I have a question for you and it's completely off the record, so I hope you don't mind my asking," Austin said. "Where are you from?"

Justice stopped for a brief moment and gave him a questioning look before falling back into step. "Why do you ask?"

"Your accent. It doesn't have a Southern drawl to it."

Justice smiled. "I'm from the Northeast. New York, actually."

"You have to be kidding me!" Austin stopped in his tracks. "I too am from New York."

"Are you serious?" Justice had a huge grin on her face.

"Yes, I was born and raised there."

"I thought I heard that Northeast in your voice, but I wasn't sure. I just knew you were not from here," Justice confirmed.

"Wow, I guess it's true what they say, it is a small world," Austin quoted someone, and they both laughed. Austin was close to her and in her space before she knew it. He reached out and pulled a strand of her hair that had fallen in her face while she was laughing.

Justice quickly popped the locks on her car. "I have to get going." She quickly threw her briefcase in the car and jumped inside. She started her car up and waved a quick good-bye, and then backed out of the driveway quickly. Stunned, Justice sped toward her house. He had touched her. And as much as she resented the touch, it had felt so good. That one brief second of his hand brushing up against her face had opened up her world. But it was wrong. He was her client. But she knew he was only being friendly and she was blowing things out of proportion.

Chapter Eight

After helping clear away the dinner dishes at her Aunt Mattie's house, Justice headed back toward the living room to sit on the couch that she loved so much. She thought she would watch a little television before heading home to read over some files. Kiki had the TV on *CSI Miami,* which was one of Justice's favorite televisions shows. The episode that was on was interesting, but her mind seemed to wander back to Austin and conversation they had the night before. She still couldn't believe they were from the same home city. How ironic. What would the odds be that they would both end up in Mississippi on the same side of the world? But what she really could not get off of her mind was his touch. His masculine hands had felt so good rubbing up against her cheek. Damn, she had to get that off of her mind. And watching *CSI* was a good way to start. But something else had been eating at her. At first she couldn't put her finger on it. All of sudden it became clear. It was Morgan. Things didn't go well with Morgan for some reason. Morgan just didn't respond to her the way she thought she would. For some reason, Morgan just didn't seem interested in anything she had asked her. She seemed distant and upset, but, after all, she was only twelve years old. And she was going through a lot, so Justice decided not to take it personally and to give her time. She just hoped Austin would go easy on her because he didn't seem to be pleased with her behavior. Trying to clear her mind so that she could focus on *CSI*, Justice was forced back to reality with Kiki yelling.

"I knew it, I knew it," Kiki testified. "Justice, didn't you think he had done it too?" Kiki asked, turning around to face her.

"Who did what?" Justice asked, startled.

"The guy killed her. The one . . ." Kiki realized, then, Justice was not watching it. "OK, give it up. What's on your mind? I can see you're not watching the show. Obviously."

"I was. I am just getting tired. I think I'm dozing." Justice faked a yawn. "I think I'll get going. I got some files to go over anyway."

"Wait. Before you leave let me tell you about my date."

"The date you had with the grocery store man?" Justice said, with a sarcastic tone.

"Yes, him." Kiki climbed off the floor where she had been seriously watching *CSI* and onto a chair across from Justice. "We met at Red Lobster for dinner which he asked me out to. But he showed up looking like he just got through working on some cars or something. And then he claimed he had a flat tire on the way over. I said, OK, fine, things happen. So we ordered our food. He ordered like two entrées for himself."

"Two?" Justice held up two fingers. "Clearly he was hungry."

"Was he! Girl, he ate all of it. And let's not even mention the cheese garlic biscuits. I think I got one out of the whole batch. He ate all the rest, Justice." Kiki twisted her face like she was sucking on a lemon.

"Wow." Justice got tickled. "OK, he was hungry, but how was the conversation?"

"Let me finish. In between him stuffing his mouth and me being disgusted, we talked. He told me that he works as a car salesman and that he didn't have any kids. I told him I worked, but for some reason I refused to tell him where. So now here comes the check!" Kiki threw her hands up in a dramatic motion. "Girl, he picked it up and looked at it, and started fumbling around for his wallet. So I continued to make small talk. That's when I realized he was trying to play me. He had the nerve to tell me he must have 'lost' his wallet when he was changing his flat tire. Then he asked me if he could 'borrow' the money to pay for the check. Justice, I almost fell out of my chair because I just knew this couldn't be happening to me—again. Another damn loser."

"So what did you do? I mean, you had to pay. You had no choice, right?"

"Hell no. I got up and told him to lose my number. I then threw the rest of my coke in his face and walked out of that restaurant."

"Kiki!" Justice said, shocked. "You could have been arrested."

"Humph, because he invited me out? And there was no way I was paying for that animal to eat," Kiki swore.

"See? Picking up men in grocery stores is not a good idea."

"I know now. And I hope they took him to jail."

"Or maybe they made him wash the dishes," Justice suggested, and they both started laughing so hard Aunt Mattie came into the living room.

"What's goin' on?" Her Southern drawl kicked in.

"Nothing. I was just telling Justice about my lousy date." Kiki slowed her laughing down. "Auntie, I just wonder when my Mr. Right gon' come along. I feel like I been waitin' forever."

"Ah, baby, you got to give it time. It'll happen. Sometimes you got to date the horrible ones to appreciate the good ones when you get 'em."

"Well, one thing for sure, I done dated all the wrong ones. So the good one got to be right around the corner. I want to meet me one of them blue-collar brothers like the one you introduced me to at the supermarket, Justice. Not him though."

"Who, Austin? Yeah, I think he could be a good guy, but I don't know." Justice shrugged her shoulder.

"Wait, who is this? What's his name again, Auston?" Aunt Mattie inquired.

"No, Auntie, it's Aus-*tin*." Justice pronounced it slowly.

"Look, Auntie, she knows, huh?" Kiki smiled. "He one of her clients, and, Auntie, he looks so good. Talk about a handsome man, he is it. And he got class." Kiki started to get real excited.

"He's all right." Justice was modest.

"Is he single?" Aunt Mattie look at Justice.

"He's divorced."

"Which means he's available," Kiki grinned. "So how often do you see him? You know, about his case."

"What do you mean how often? He's my client. I have to see him only to consult," Justice answered nonchalantly. "So are you still working all that overtime?" She tried to change the subject.

"I knew you were holding something back. That's why you weren't paying attention to *CSI*. You love that show, and nothing ever takes away your attention." Kiki studied Justice as if she could read her thoughts. "It's about Austin, isn't it? Tell me, tell me now." Kiki sat on the edge of her seat.

"There is nothing to tell. He is my client, so I met with him Friday . . . at his house," Justice procrastinated. "But only because of his daughter. She's twelve, and we wanted her to be comfortable meeting with me about the case. So he thought this would be the best environment." Justice fidgeted in her seat.

"Oh my God, Auntie," Kiki yelled. "You two had a date. Justice had a date with the hunk of the century." Kiki jumped out of her chair.

"Kiki, it was not a date. It was a client-attorney consultation."

"Did you guys eat anything?"

"Yeah, he made dinner. But only to make things normal for his daughter," Justice convinced herself. "Aunt Mattie, do you think it's wrong? I agreed because of his daughter."

"No, baby, it's not wrong. You have to do what your job requires; his daughter was there so it's respectable. You did right to go." Auntie Mattie continued to use her Southern drawl.

"How was it? Can he at least cook?" Kiki was grinning so hard her cheeks flushed.

"Yes, he is a good cook."

"What does his house look like? I know it's the bomb, right? A man like that don't live in no junk crib." Kiki rolled her neck.

"Right again. It was beautiful. I mean, he has some very good taste. I was surprised. I thought I would walk into an all-black leather pad man cave. I mean, that's normally the furniture bachelors have."

"I'm not surprised. I told you he was a good guy."

"The verdict is not in on that one. But I think he is ." Justice shrugged her shoulder pretending to be uninterested in the conversation.

"Oh, Justice, you're so lucky. Give your cousin a hug." Kiki rushed over and gave Justice a huge hug. "Now you go and get your husband." Kiki sprinted out of the room before Justice could contest. She looked at Aunt Mattie.

"Auntie, it's not like that." Justice tried again to convince her.

"Oh, baby, don't you pay your cousin no mind, ya hear?"

Justice sank back into the couch and let out a huge sigh. And when she wasn't paying attention Aunt Mattie smiled. She knew what Justice herself didn't even know. Her heart was already in it. It was written all over her face.

Chapter Nine

"What's up, man? You still haven't told me how the meeting went with Justice. I know I unexpectedly disappeared this weekend. But the week is almost over. What's up?" Trent rolled his chair toward Austin's desk with a bubbling hot cup of Folgers coffee.

Austin watched the coffee cup, afraid Trent might spill it on him. "Can you be careful with that lethal cup of coffee?" Austin slid his chair back an inch.

"Don't worry, I got this." Trent sipped and smiled. "Answer the question."

"Ah, man, she's great. She already arranged temporary custody."

"Really? Man, I told she was bad."

"Yeah, she is that." Austin had a glint in his eyes. "Man, have you ever seen her before?"

"Nah, I never seen her. As much as she has been on the news for winning cases I never catch her picture. Why?"

"I just asked. She's quite a woman."

"Wait a minute. She *must* be fine. I can see it in your eyes, man," Trent laughed.

"She is absolutely stunning. To say 'fine' would be to downplay her. Man, she is the total package. She is elegant, daring, and beautiful. I can't explain it, but she is a real woman." Austin stared into space. He realized Trent was staring at him. He didn't mean to go this deep; he just wanted to express his thoughts of Justice in a truthful and respectable way. "Uhh . . ." Austin cleared his throat. "She is, you know, good for the case."

"Austin, my brother, my brother, are you in love with this woman?" Trent grinned from ear to ear.

"No . . . I, uh . . . No," Austin stumbled. "But thank you for recommending her to me."

"Ah, man, you got it *bad*," Trent laughed. "But it's OK. Just don't forget about the case." Trent continued to laugh.

"Come on with the laughing. She is here for me and Morgan. I just think she's nice. That's it. A clean client-and-attorney relationship. She came over last week."

"She *what?*" Trent dropped the file in his hand.

"For Morgan. See, she told me that she would have to speak with Morgan about the case. So I invited her over to the house so that Morgan would be comfortable. And since we normally eat dinner about that time I invited her to eat as well." Austin stirred in his seat.

"Well, I'm *sure* it went well." Trent continued to laugh. "I'm just mad you didn't invite me," he joked.

"Ah, you got jokes," Austin grinned. "Shut up, man. Just shut up." Austin stood up at his desk and grabbed a file. "Come on. Let's go in here and question this witness."

"All right, all right." Trent tried to clean up his laugh while he straightened his tie. "You ask him the hard questions, and I'll play the nice one."

"Cool," Austin replied.

They headed toward the interrogation room. Trent still wore a grin on his face. Austin secretly started to wonder if he had, in fact, had an agenda for inviting Justice over. Why didn't he just invite her out to meet him and Morgan at a restaurant? He had tried to convince himself that it could only remain business between them, but there was just something about her that made his heart race. When he saw her at the door at his house he had wanted to greet her with a passionate kiss. But he kicked himself for having such thoughts. And when he had walked her out to her car and she had laughed and gave that beautiful captivating smile that he was sure she didn't even know she possessed, he almost could not contain himself from touching her. He had lain in bed all night regretting it. He knew it was totally out of line. What if she decided to drop the case because of it? There would be no way he could ever forgive himself. Justice was his only chance at getting full custody of Morgan. And that is why he would apologize to her as soon as he figured out what to say.

ðð ð

Justice picked up her buzzing phone.

"Justice, Mr. Rhem is on his way in to see you."

"Thanks." Justice hung up the phone right when Mr. Rhem tapped on her door.

"How are you, Justice?" he asked as he approached her desk.

"Afternoon, Mr. Rhem." Justice stood up to greet him with her right hand outstretched. "Have a seat."

Mr. Rhem took a seat and unbuttoned the jacket to his suit, which was undeniably Tommy Hilfiger. Mr. Rhem was white. He stood about 5 foot 7 and weighed 180 pounds. At 52 years old, he was still a pretty nice-looking guy. He had a reputation of having a hard edge, being a no-nonsense type of guy. But on all accounts he was fair, regardless of race. Justice appreciated that about him, being in the South and of mixed race. This could pose a problem in the workplace. But so far, Mr. Rhem and Mr. Garrett had been fair to her. They treated her nothing less than equal.

"So what brings you in today?" Justice inquired in a professional tone.

"I had something I needed to discuss with you. Garret wanted to be here, but as you know, he got called out to Las Vegas on business."

"Yes, I'm aware."

"Since you have been here, you have done a wonderful job. You have kicked ass in the entire state of Mississippi. And there is no way we could ever thank you," Mr. Rhem said in his Southern drawl. He spoke very clearly. Even after living in Mississippi since the age of eight, Justice had never lost her New York City accent. And she still found it funny when she would hear Southerners speak. She enjoyed it. But she wondered where this conversation was going. Was she being fired? After all, like he had just said, she has kicked ass all over Mississippi for this firm. So why on earth would they want to let her go? "Again, Garret hated that he couldn't be here for this. But I assured him that I would take care of it."

Justice just couldn't take anymore. She would not be fired. She would not take this sitting down with a smile. "Mr. Rhem, where are you going with this?" Her voice stayed steady. She would not let him know that she was shaking with fear.

"Well, Justice, do you remember that court in New York that you asked Garrett and myself to give you a letter a recommendation for? They responded back. They want you," Mr. Rhem spilled.

Justice sat stock-still. She couldn't move. She was not sure if she heard him right.

"Did you hear me, Justice? That court would like to have you as a first pick to be a judge. They are pulling out all the stops to get you."

"Are you sure?" Justice asked in shock. "I mean, it's only been a week since I applied."

"You came highly recommended. They couldn't pass you up. Your record speaks volumes. And I just want to congratulate you."

"Thank you, Mr. Rhem," Justice replied, wanting to scream with excitement but holding back.

"Somehow I thought you would be more excited." Mr. Rhem seemed concerned.

"Oh, I am excited. But I need time to digest this. It's very surreal, sir," Justice explained. "I actually thought you were about to fire me."

"Fire you? Justice, whatever for? This firm wouldn't fire you even if you committed a serious crime. You are one of the best things that ever happen to this firm. Frankly, we hate to see you leave. However, we don't want to stand in front of your dream. We know how much this means to you. To be so young you are very dedicated. We wish you luck." Mr. Rhem stood up.

"Again, thank you, Mr. Rhem." Justice stood and gave him another handshake.

Justice didn't know what to do when Mr. Rhem left her office, she was so elated. The palms of her hands started to sweat from excitement and a hint of nervousness took over in the pit of her stomach. Who should she tell first? Of course, Aunt Mattie and Kiki. She reached to pick up her phone, but quickly decided against telling them over the phone. Telling them in person would be better. She grabbed her purse and keys and headed out of the office.

She pulled into Aunt Mattie's driveway and noticed right away that Kiki's car was absent. That's when she remembered Kiki was pulling another double today for Deloris. But her mind was made up. Kiki would have to find out later. She had to tell someone, or she would just burst. Justice put her key into the front door and turned the knob. The living room was quiet. The television was off and all the living-room drapes were still drawn, which was unusual. Auntie Mattie always kept the drapes open to catch any sign bit of daylight.

"Auntie?" Justice yelled out, her voice was full of excitement. With no answer from her aunt, Justice headed down the hallway toward the kitchen. "Auntie, are you ho—" Justice entered the kitchen shocked to see her aunt sitting at the kitchen table. She knew immediately something was wrong because just as she entered the kitchen she saw Auntie Mattie quickly try to dry a tear from her clearly disturbed face.

"What's the matter?" A concerned look came over Justice's face and a gripping knot entered her stomach.

"Nothing, baby. Just not feeling well. I think I need to take a nap."

"You had a doctor's appointment today, didn't you?" With all the excitement Justice had forgotten that Aunt Mattie had a doctor's appointment earlier in the day. She secretly kicked herself for forgetting. "What did the doctor say? You are OK, right?" Justice's heart slowed waiting for a response.

"You know I ain't been feeling well lately. Doctor Turnpike says I have lupus, and it's affecting my diabetes. He wants me to take it really easy. He's considering putting me on bed rest. My blood pressure is through the roof according to him. He threatens to put me in the hospital if he doesn't see any improvement next week."

"Auntie . . ." Justice said, as tears leaked down her face.

"Oh, Justice, now you stop that. I'ma be fine. I'll continue to take my medication, and I'll rest just like the doctor ordered. I'll be fine." Aunt Mattie reached across the table and grabbed both of Justice's hands. "Now you wipe those tears." Aunt Mattie smiled like she always did, being strong for her family. But Justice knew this wasn't good. "Now, what did you want to tell me?" Aunt Mattie took a sip from the cup that she was nursing in front of her. Justice knew it was coffee from the steam and the smell that hit her when she entered the kitchen.

"What?" Justice asked, almost forgetting why she had come over.

"You sounded cheerful when you came through the door. I just figured you had something good to tell me."

"Oh no. I just stopped by. I had a free moment at the office," Justice lied. There was just no way she would tell her that she was moving to New York. Not while she was sick. There was no way she could up and move at a time like this. Her aunt needed her, and she would be there for her the same way she had been there for Justice when she needed her.

"Are you sure? I didn't ruin any surprises you had for me, did I?"

"Surprise? No." Justice forced a smile.

"You're not getting married, are you? Because that would cure me for sure." Aunt Mattie started to laugh.

"No. What on earth would make you think that?" Justice gave her a sincere smile. "I'm not even dating, Auntie."

"Well, I had to ask." Aunt Mattie took another sip from her cup and continued to smile.

Chapter Ten

Justice and Kiki had decided to meet up at Starbucks to discuss Aunt Mattie's illness. Justice had arrived a few minutes before Kiki. She was still contemplating if she should tell Kiki about her promotion. She worried that Kiki would slip up and tell Aunt Mattie. And the last thing she wanted was for Aunt Mattie to feel guilty about her rethinking going to New York.

Justice saw Kiki finally come through the Starbucks door. She watched her head straight to the counter to order her latte. Justice took a sip of her latte as she tried to calm herself for the conversation. She had been having migraine headaches back to back since Aunt Mattie had given her the news. A migraine was threatening her sanity at that very moment, but she was refusing to let it take control.

"Hey." Kiki reached down and gave Justice a hug after she had placed her cup on the table.

"Hi," Justice answered back. She didn't realize how much she had needed that hug until Kiki released her hold.

"So how have you been holding up since Auntie gave you the news?" Kiki asked before sipping from her cup.

"I don't even know that I have been holding up," Justice admitted. "One thing is for sure though, the migraines came back in full force."

"Really? I'm sorry to hear that. You need to make sure that you take it easy." Kiki had a huge concerned look on her face. She was worried about her cousin.

"What about you?" Justice questioned. "Are you going to be all right?"

"Yeah, I am. Just trying to stay strong for Auntie. I took a day off the other day. When I went into work I told them that all those extra hours got to cease. At least until Auntie is better."

"We have to make sure that she's taking her medicine. No excuses. And she needs to exercise to help with the diabetes. I called up a personnel trainer that will come by the house like three days a week to make sure that she is at least getting a half-hour workout three days a week."

"Personnel trainer?" Kiki said shocked. "Girl, you will be lucky if she even lets that trainer into the house. You know how she is when it comes to discipline, especially some trainer."

"I know. I thought about that but it's at least worth a try. She needs her exercise, and a trainer will give her just the motivation she needs. At least I hope so," Justice smiled.

"Well, I guess we'll see." Kiki sipped from her cup. They both sat for a moment in silence savoring the taste of their lattes. Starbucks had the best, and they were indeed addicted.

"I was offered a position as a judge," Justice blurted out.

"Justice, that's what's up," Kiki smiled. "We have to celebrate. It's time to party." Kiki snapped her fingers. "While we sitting here having lattes we should be toasting with vodka." Kiki noticed Justice wasn't smiling. "Justice, what's the matter? You just told me that you're about to become a judge. And correct me if I am wrong, but that was your goal."

"The job is in New York."

"New York?" Kiki repeats leaving her mouth open wide enough for flies to enter. "New York is good. It's where you come from, and most importantly, there are lots of fun things to do. Oh, wait, you *hate* fun. Now I see your problem," Kiki joked, but Justice did not laugh.

"Can't you see there is no way I can move to New York, not now?"

"And why not?"

"Aunt Mattie needs me. She needs both of us. I can't just go running off to New York." Justice shook her head.

"Wait! ou haven't told her about the job, have you?"

"No, and I'm not going to. Right now, she needs to focus on her health not my career. If I tell her, she will feel guilty about me staying."

"Justice, if you tell her, she is going to want you to go. If you don't tell her, she will never forgive you for keeping it from her."

"Just like I got that offer I will get another one. I'll just stay here and wait for a position to come open here."

"Yeah, right, like they gon' make a young black womn in Mississippi a judge over the twenty white males that's applying for it."

"Kiki, not all things are about race. Now, I have managed to come a long way at the firm. And neither my race nor my skin color have been an issue. Surely I can secure a position as a judge," Justice said with confidence.

"Humph, well, I wouldn't hold my breath." Kiki sipped from her cup.

"Kiki, what do you expect me to do? Be selfish and just worry about myself and what I want? Because I can't do that." Justice's eyes watered with tears so she took a napkin and dabbed around her eyes to keeping from ruining her makeup.

"The selfish part will be you not telling Aunt Mattie. She has a right to know that your dream is coming true. If you don't tell her, she will blame herself forever. So you can't do that to her." Kiki looked her dead in the eyes. "Justice, can't you see this will make her proud? She is going to be happy. She would never keep you here. Besides, she has me. I will always take care of her. I love her too, remember?"

"I know," Justice sniffled.

"I love you, cousin, and I want to see you happy. You deserve it." Kiki got up from the table and walked over to give Justice a hug.

"I love you too," Justice smiled. "And thanks for being there. But you can't tell Auntie. Let me tell her."

"OK, I will," Kiki agree as she sat back down in her chair.

"And on my time." Justice stressed that part. Kiki smiled and starteds to finish up her .

"Hi, Justice." Justice turned toward the voice that she knew all too well.

"Clay, what are you doing here?" Justice seemed to interrogate.

"Just grabbing some coffee," Clay answered, but Justice noticed he hadn't taken his eyes off of Kiki since he approached the table.

"Clay, this is my cousin Kiki. Kiki, this is Clay. He's an attorney with Schuster and Bell law firm."

"Hi, Kiki." Clay smiled from ear to ear.

"Hey" Kiki spoke nonchalantly.

"Although I really hate to, I got to run. Justice, you know how it is; court is calling. Kiki, it was a pleasure meeting you. And I'm sure we'll meet again." And just like that, Clay strolled off with a glint in his eyes without even saying goodbye to Justice.

Justice watched Clay as he left Starbucks in a daze. "Did you see that?" Justice asked Kiki referring to Clay.

"See what?" Kiki seemed confused.

"Clay was all over you. Kiki, he likes you. I mean, he *really* likes you."

"That guy? No, I doubt it." Kiki shrugged her shoulders.

"Trust me, he likes you."

"Justice, there is no way a guy like that would be interested in a woman like me. He's an attorney, for God's sake. I work for Wal-Mart. We have *nothing* in common."

"First off, there is no such thing as a woman like you. Kiki, you are a beautiful person. Any man would be lucky to have you. Second, where you work does not define you. And the first man that can't accept that, you tell him to kiss your ass. Now, as I was saying earlier, Clay likes you. Couldn't you tell he was flirting?" Justice grinned.

"Flirting, no, but a little odd . . . maybe, with all that 'Kiki, it was a pleasure meeting you.'" Kiki mocked Clay, and she and Justice both laughed.

ðð ð

Austin was shocked to receive the call from Tabitha that Justice was requesting to see him and Morgan in her office. So right after picking Morgan up from school, they headed straight over to Garrett & Rhem. He was still nervous about seeing her because he still had not had time to apologize to her. Morgan was quiet on the ride over, which gave him plenty of time to be nervous, so by the time they stepped off the elevator leading to Tabitha's desk, he had finally started to calm down.

"Hi, Mr. Crews," Tabitha greeted him as soon as they approached her desk.

"Hi, Tabitha," Austin replied.

"And this beautiful young lady must be Morgan," Tabitha complimented Morgan and extended her hand to her. And to Austin's surprise, Morgan smiled.

"Yes, I'm Morgan." Morgan reached her hand out to shake Tabitha's hand.

Tabitha picked up the phone on her mahogany desk and alerted Justice of their arrival. "OK, you can head right in. She's ready for you." Tabitha pointed toward at the door leading to Justice's office.

Before Austin could open the door it swung open with Justice directly on the other end of it. "Good evening, Austin, come right in. Hi, Morgan."

"Good evening to you, Ms. Justice," Austin smiled. It was all he could do to not reach out and kiss her smack-dab on the lips. God, she looked beautiful, sexy, and downright irresistible. The design was unknown to Austin, but Justice had on Dolce Gabbana cuffed pants with the matching wool jacket. Underneath the jacket her body supported a solid Crepe de Chine blouse with a pair of pony hair suede pumps. All Austin knew was that she looked stunning. He was so caught up into her beauty that he didn't notice that Morgan hadn't returned Justice's greeting.

Justice offered them a seat as she made her way back to her chair parked directly in front of the desk. She again brushed off the fact Morgan didn't speak when she entered the office. Her mission today was to get right down to business. Time was winding down; time was of the essence, and she intended to settle this with Austin having full custody of his daughter.

"OK, let's get right down to it. Morgan, I still have some things that I need to discuss with you." Justice positioned herself in an upward position. "Morgan, you understand that this custody mean you will permanently live with your dad. And at this point, your mother will not even have visitation rights. How does this make you feel?"

Without even uttering a sound Morgan gave Justice a blank stare.

"Morgan, Justice is asking you a question," Austin said.

"Hmmm," Morgan took in a deep breath. "I understand what it all means," was Morgan's reply. At this point, she didn't have anything to say to Justice. She saw the way her dad looked at Justice every time they got together. And it made her upset. She was starting to feel as if this was not about her. Her dad paid no attention to her when Justice was around. She felt unimportant, and more than anything, she just wanted to leave that office.

At that moment Justice saw the hurt in Morgan's eyes. Something was bothering her. Austin had warned her that Morgan had been through a lot. She missed her mother, and she just wasn't up for these sessions. But Justice had to find some way to get through to her because in the end, it would be for the best. Justice was no counselor, but she was a damn good attorney, and she would continue to try to get through to Morgan so she tried a different approach.

"Morgan, I know right now that things are not looking good for you. I understand that this is a lot, all these questions and talk about custody. But this is an important part of the process. Without it, we could fail. But I'm sure all of us sitting here are here for one reason and one reason only. And that's the success of gaining full custody to keep you home with your dad."

Austin looked at Justice in amazement and nodded his head in agreement. Justice was an amazing woman, and what she said was very well put.

Morgan had again seen that look in his eyes when he looked at Justice, and this just upset her more. Everything Justice had just said was untrue. It wasn't about her. It was about them two wanting to be together. She was twelve but no fool. Her dad may have hung on to Justice's every word, but she would not.

"You are wrong, because you don't anything about me or my mother. And I don't want to talk about it," Morgan spit out and folded her arms. Her chest heaved up and down so fast it was clear that she was close to tears.

"Morgan!" Austin said in pure shock. He sat up on the edge of his chair. "You apologize to Justice right now. She's an adult, and more importantly, she is here to help us."

Morgan knew by the sound of her father's voice that he meant business; he never scolded her. "I'm sorry," she mumbled, not meaning one word of it.

"It's OK, sweetheart," Justice said.

"Justice, I am so sorry for Morgan's rude behavior. I don't know what has gotten into her. I know time is wasting, but I would like to reschedule this. I need to have a talk with Morgan."

"Just give Tabitha a call in the next couple of days and have her set it up," Justice said. Morgan stood up and left the office.

"Again, Justice, I am sorry. I promise I will take care of this. It will not happen again. Thanks for having patience." With that Austin left the office where he found Morgan standing at the elevator. They rode the elevator down in silence. They got inside Austin's squad car. He started the car and almost pulled off, but he shut the engine off instead.

"Pumpkin, what's going on? Why would you say those things to Justice? iIt's just not like you. So tell me what's really bothering you," Austin pried.

"Nothing, Dad." Morgan shifted her body facing the window. "I just want to go home and get in bed."

"Morgan, look at me," Austin instructed her. "Now, I want to know what's going on. This is the not the first time you were short with Justice. You had the same behavior when she came over to the house. I thought maybe you behaved that way because you were uncomfortable with the meeting. But what just happened back there displays something else. Now I need to know what's bothering you. Is it about your mother, because if it is, we can talk about that."

Morgan wiped the tears off her face and tried to control her breathing to hide the fact that she was crying. "Do you like her, Dad?"

"Who, Pumpkin?" Austin asked confused.

"Her. Ms. Justice." Morgan shook her head. "I've seen the way you look at her, and I've never seen you look at other women like that."

Shocked, Austin could barely find the words to answer. He couldn't believe she knew. Had she been watching him, or was it really that obvious?

"I, umm, umm, well, I like her as a friend." Austin tried to sound casual instead of shocked. But the shock was clearly in his stumbling voice.

"Do you think she's pretty?"

"Yes, I think she is pretty and nice."

"I figured that. It's like when she is around, you forget all about me, and I can't ever remember you being like that over Mom. And I'm afraid she'll make you forget all about me." Morgan wiped more tears off her wet face.

"Sweetheart, don't you know that could never happen? No one, and I mean *no one*, could ever make me forget about you. You are my little angel. That's why I'm fighting so hard to get custody of you."

"Really?" Morgan turned to face her father. "Do you pinkie swear it?" She held up her pinkie finger.

"I pinkie swear." Austin held up his finger and reached out and hugged Morgan really tight.

"Now," Austin sat straight up facing the steering wheel, "we'll be going to court pretty soon. It's some weeks away, but it will be here before we know it. So, Justice still needs to go over some things with you. It is very important that we get this done. And in order to do that, you have to cooperate with her. OK?"

"OK."

"Can you do that for me?"

"Yes, Dad. And I am so sorry for the way I behaved. I was awful, wasn't I? She probably thinks you raised a monster." Morgan laughed but sniffled from the crying she had done.

"I wouldn't say you were that awful." Austin smiled. "But Justice is a very understanding person. She is going to help us out a lot. So you just work with her to make the process easy."

"OK."

Austin started the car up and gave his daughter a big smile. "Are you hungry?" he asked.

"Yeah, I could eat."

"How does Sonic sound?"

"A greasy burger with chili cheese fries. Anytime, Dad," Morgan said with a grin.

Chapter Eleven

Justice had just gotten out of the shower when her cell phone started to vibrate, and to her surprise, Austin's name popped up. She had programmed his number into her phone just the day before. She instantly wondered what he could want on a Saturday, but without hesitation, she answered on the second vibrate. To her amazement, he had asked if she could meet him for lunch to discuss some issues. Since she didn't have any plans besides curling up on her couch with a cup of hot cocoa and reading some case files that she had come across that had been tried at the Supreme Court on segregation, those cases always sparked her interest—she could sit and read them for hours—she decided to take Austin to up on his offer.

She had been feeling energized since her six-mile run with Kiki that morning. On their run, Kiki had informed her that she had run into Clay at Walmart, and he had asked her out for a date. With all that excitement on her mind, Justice wondered, why not? Austin had decided on the Hunan House, a local upscale Chinese restaurant not too far from where Justice lived. So she quickly headed to her closet and pulled out a pair of Phil Lim-draped pocket trousers with a red haute black cowl-neck tank top and a pair of all-black suede Prada pumps. With one last glance in the mirror she decided that she looked presentable. She popped two Extra Strength Excedrin pills in her mouth to beat the migraine before it decided to invade and headed out the front door.

By the time she pulled her all-black Range Rover with all-black rims into the parking lot of the restaurant, she could see that Austin had already arrived. Pulling in beside his black Escalade, Justice jumped out of her truck, hit the alarm, and strutted inside. The waitress led her to the table where Austin stood and greeted her, then pulled out her chair for her to sit down.

Again, Austin was totally mesmerized by Justice. She walked into the restaurant looking flawless. He had invited her to lunch to apologize for touching her at his house, but seeing her only made him want to touch her again and not just brush a strand of hair out of her face. He wanted to wrap his arms around her waist and whisper in her ear, but instead, he greeted her and politely pulled out her chair.

"Hi," Austin spoke.

"Hey," Justice returned as she sat down in her seat.

"I picked this restaurant because Chinese is one of my favorites. And they have like the best."

"Actually, I love Chinese food too, so you made a good choice."

"Wow, again, you shock me." Austin smiled. "So I know you are wondering why I invited you out to lunch." Austin was cut off by the waitress who took their order as another waitress delivered the wine that he had preordered.

"Can I pour you a glass of this?" Austin referred to the wine.

"Sure," Justice answered.

Austin started pouring the wine in her glass, and it sparkled. "Really sparkly, huh?" he said referring to the wine.

"Yeah, it is."

"OK, back to why I invited you out to lunch. And I hope you don't think it's too much, but it's just lunch."

"Austin, it's OK. You can relax. What's up?" Justice tried to get to the point.

"I invited you to lunch for two reasons. One, to apologize for touching you. That was completely out of line, and I'm sorry. I don't want to do anything to make you uncomfortable and jeopardize our client-lawyer relationship." Austin was sincere.

"Well, your apology is accepted and don't sweat it." Justice took a sip of her wine.

"Second, I want to again apologize for Morgan's behavior."

"Austin, I told you not to worry about that. I understand that she is going through a lot."

"I know, but her talking to you in that manner was unacceptable. But I talked to her, and we got to the bottom of things." Austin got quiet again as the waitress placed their food on the tables. After making sure they didn't need anything the waitress left.

"Wow, this looks good." Justice's eyes wandered the table, examining the different dishes. But she paused on her favorite dish, Spicy Orange Chicken with Broccoli.

"Well, eat as much as you want. I won't judge you," Austin laughed.

"Thanks." Justice smiled as she took a bite into her orange chicken. "As you were about to say . . ."

"We talked, and she's ready to talk with you now."

"I knew she would come around. We just needed to give her time."

"She really misses Monica. Every time she runs off like this, Morgan misses her for a while and just as she starts to get over it, Monica reappears. And that's why I have to stop her."

"Is she from here, Monica? Is she from Gulfport?"

"Yeah. I met her when I first moved here. I used to work out at the YMCA, and she used to train there. She was like a professional swimmer around the states."

"Wow, really?"

"Yep, and we got married not long after meeting and right away she got pregnant with Morgan. Right from the start Monica was restless. She always wanted to travel and do things. But it was hard for me because I had just moved here where I was promoted to lead detective, so my plate was full. I was spending sometimes twenty-two-hour-days at the office. She complained about it at first, so I got her a nanny so that she would have help with Morgan and still be able to go out and feel free.

"But soon that wasn't enough. She started showing up at my job in a rage over me being at work. Telling me she couldn't take any more so I cut back on my hours and took her on vacation. I thought things were getting better. Then I come home from work one day, and the nanny tells me that

Monica packed her bags and just left. She told the nanny that she was going away for a while and that she would be back. I was outraged. I couldn't believe it. Morgan was only two years old at the time, and her mother had just packed up and left. Like she was going on a picnic. I just couldn't believe it.

"She stayed gone for four months. When she came back she was all apologetic and we went to marriage counseling and tried to fix it. But not even a full two years later she did it again. Once again, I was in shock but when she came back that time she stayed put until we got a divorce years later. Then one year after the divorce she did it again. She dropped Morgan off for one of our weekends, then took off. And she has been doing it ever since. I'm just fed up. Enough is enough. My baby deserves better," Austin said getting caught up in his words. He almost forgot he was talking to Justice.

"I think you are doing the right thing," Justice spoke up.

"Oh, I'm sorry. I didn't mean to go on like that. I just got caught up." Austin apologized after realizing he was going on and on.

"It's OK. That's a pretty interesting story. I'm glad you told me."

"No doubt. But Morgan is good. She's ready to talk to you. So I'll call Tabitha on Monday and set something up for this week."

"Cool, I'll clear my calendar."

"I'll have to work around her swimming lessons, but I'm sure we can work it out."

"Oh, she's a swimmer too?"

"I signed her up for lessons awhile ago, and now she's a pro. Her coach is really impressed. She practices like three days a week."

"That's good." Justice took a sip of her wine and came up with an idea. "I tell you what, how about I pick her up from her swimming lessons one day this week? I'll take her out for a bite to eat and we'll talk. I promise to bring her home right after."

"You sure you don't mind picking her up?" Austin asked.

"It will be no problem. It will be good for both of us."

"All right, just let me know what day and I'll tell her to look out for you."

"I think I have eaten enough," Justice said.

"Well, I don't think I've eaten anything. I've been talking way too much," he joked.

After talking for a little while longer Justice decided she had to go. She needed to get home and do some reading. Sunday she would be busy with her auntie, and Monday was back to work so she had to make sure she had some time to read. She loved it, and when she missed it, it messed up her whole week. But lunch with Austin had been informing and relaxing. She had enjoyed herself.

ððð

"What's going on with you? You haven't said much since you picked me up," Auntie Mattie gave Justice a concerned look while she squeezed her foot into a pair of Liz Claiborne red pumps.

"I'm fine. I just been thinking about Mom lately. I really miss her."

"I miss her too, baby. She would be so proud of you, Justice. You set out to do everything she wanted to do," Aunt Mattie grinned.

"I know. If it hadn't been for her I don't know what career path I might have chosen."

"Baby, you would have been a lawyer. You own it; it's your true passion. Ya mother, well, she just brought it out in you," Aunt Mattie said in a soothing tone. Justice loved talking to her aunt. She could smooth any wrinkle in Justice's day. And she needed this day of shopping with Aunt Mattie.

"So how have you been feeling this week?" Justice asked.

"I been feeling just fine. Just trying to get used to that new blood pressure medicine the doctor put me on. But I'm fine, baby."

"It's not making you feel sick, is it? Because if it is, you need to let your doctor know."

"Ah, no, I'm fine. I just have to adjust to it." Aunt Mattie waved her hand as the saleslady approached to see if the shoes fit. "Look here, I want you to bring this in a bigger size. Either my feet are bigger or they're swollen," Aunt Mattie said to the saleslady with a slight laugh.

"Yes, ma'am," the saleslady said and gathered up the shoes to return them to the back of the storeroom.

"Auntie, your feet do look a little swollen. Are you sure you feel all right?"

"Justice, baby, I'm fine. You worry yourself too much. Now, ain't nothin' wrong wit' my feet, except maybe I should elevate them more. But I'm fine. Now stop all that frettin' over me, ya hear?"

"OK, Auntie, I'll try." Justice smiled as she sat down beside her.

"Now what's this Kiki tells me about you being offered a job as a judge in New York?" Aunt Mattie said. Justice stood up in shock.

"She told you that? I can't believe her. I specifically asked her not to." Justice started to get angry.

"Of course she told me, and how could you not tell me? Is that how I raised you, to keep something as important as that from me? And don't get upset with Kiki. She just loves you. And just like me, she wants the best for you." Justice could see the hurt in her eyes.

"I'm not mad at her. And I had planned to tell yo—" Justice waited for the saleslady to give the shoe box to her aunt. Finally the woman walked away. "I was going to tell you, but I had to figure out how without upsetting you. It's really not a big deal. There will be other opportunities."

Aunt Mattie put the shoes down to face Justice. "You listen to me. I have worked too hard and loved you too much to watch you throw away your dream. I'm fine, and I need you to believe me when I say that. You have given up your whole life to prove that you are worthy of this job. I have watched you work day in and day out to achieve this. And I will *not* stand by and watch you toss it out the window like it was a bag of chips. Now, I want you to go to New York and continue to make me proud."

"But, Auntie—" Justice tried to protest.

"Uh-uh. No ifs, ands, or buts. You are going. And I will be in New York for your first trial to watch you walk out in that robe and sit on that bench." Aunt Mattie smiled with certainty.

"I love you, Auntie." Justice walked over and gave her a huge hug.

"I better try on this shoe before that saleslady thinks I don't intend on buying anything. By the way, your cousin is really excited about that guy you introduced her to."

"Who, Clay?"

"I think that's his name. Maybe he's the one for her."

"He's a good guy."

"I hope so, because that is exactly what she needs. That's what both of you need."

Justice just smiled. She didn't even want to have the relationship-marriage conversation with her aunt. In her mind, she was done with the marriage thing. Career was number one in her book or list of things to achieve.

"I got to get both of you to the altar. So you better put your dating shoes back on too. I'ma walk both of y'all down that aisle. I done promised myself that. So you better get to gettin'."

"I have to meet someone first, Auntie," Justice smiled.

"Ah, baby, don't worry about that. You already have," Aunt Mattie informed her.

"Who?" Justice questioned.

Saundra

Deciding not to answer Justice, Aunt Mattie slid her feet into the second pair of red pumps, and they fit just perfectly. She knew she only needed a bigger size, and after all that fuss Justice was making about her feet, it was just plain nonsense. She was fine, and so were her feet. Or at least she would be as soon as that blood pressure medicine started to work. Once the medicine kicked in, she would be feeling one hundred percent better.

Chapter Twelve

"May I help you?" Morgan's coach approached a wandering Justice in the hallway.

"Yes. I am looking for Morgan Crews. I came to pick her up."

"Well, you are close. She is right this way." The coach turned and opened a door up on the right side of the hall. Once the door was open Justice could hear all the noise coming from the room, the swishing of the water and a loud whistle constantly blowing.

"She's still in the water. I'll let her know you're here."

"Thanks," Justice said as she looked in the direction of the swimmers and locked eyes with Morgan, who just noticed Justice and gave her a slight smile.

Morgan spoke with her coach for a brief moment, then grabbed her towel and climbed out of the pool. Justice took in a deep relaxing breath as she watched Morgan head her way.

"Hi," Justice said as soon as Morgan stopped in front of her.

"Hey," Morgan replied.

"I'm sure your dad told you I would be picking you up," Justice smiled.

"Yeah, he told me. I need to get dressed. Why don't you hang out here, and I'll be right back?"

"Take your time," Justice encouraged her as Morgan walked toward the dressing room.

Justice turned toward the wall with pictures of past swimmers. As she walked the wall looking at the pictures she saw picture of a woman who resembled Morgan a lot. And under the picture she read the name. "Monica." *So that must be Morgan's mother. Austin said she had been a professional swimmer.* And as Justice continued to walk the wall she saw about five more pictures of Monica.

"I'm ready." Morgan startled Justice she had approached her from behind.

"You're ready? So how about we go for pizza," Justice suggested.

"Cool." Morgan adjusted her backpack on her right shoulder.

Justice started up the ignition once inside the car. "So which pizza place do you prefer? Pizza Hut, Papa John, which one do you like?"

"Actually, my favorite is Sal's Pizzeria."

"Then Sal's Pizzeria it is." Justice gave Morgan an approving nod as she put the truck in drive. As they pulled into Sal's, Justice noticed there were a lot of cars, which meant there must be a crowd. She pulled her Range Rover into a parking space close to the entrance.

Finding a seat was easier than Justice thought it would be judging from the cars outside. The waitress seated them and took their order right away since Morgan knew without a doubt what she wanted. And to her surprise, it was the same thing Justice wanted. They both discovered that pepperoni was their favorite.

"So how was practice today?" Justice inquired, deciding to break the ice without starting right in with her questions about the custody battle.

"It was fun. I always enjoy myself."

"That's good. Do you compete?" Justice asked.

"Well, I wouldn't call it competing, but Coach does make me do a race twice weekly."

"Your dad told me you were good."

"I wouldn't say all that, but I do OK," Morgan said. "My mom used to compete; she actually was a professional. That's what sparked my interest to learn to swim. She had tried to get me to learn for a long time, but I refused." Morgan looked up at the waitress who brought her a Diet Coke. "Thanks."

"So what made you change your mind?" Justice stirred her drink.

"I, uh . . ." Morgan stalled staring into her drink. "I, uh . . . Well, I was kind of afraid of all the water." Morgan seemed embarrassed.

"That sounds normal to me," Justice chuckled. "I didn't learn to swim until I went off to college. And it wasn't that I did not want to learn. But it took me that long to build up the courage."

Morgan gave her a huge grin. "Are you any good at it?" she questioned.

"Let's just say I won't drown," Justice smiled.

The waitress brought the pizza to the table and gave it a spin. That was sort of a ritual at Sal's. Morgan always thought it gave the pizza that extra good taste.

"Looks delicious," Justice complimented to the waitress.

"Do you need anything?" the waitress asked.

Justice looked at Morgan who shook her head for no.

"Enjoy," the waitress said and spun around toward the kitchen.

Morgan reached for a slice of piping hot pizza and took a big bite. "This is good," she said with her mouth full.

Justice smiled at her. "I'm glad you like it." She reached for a slice of pizza. "So are you enjoying living with your dad?"

"Yeah, he takes good care of me."

"Soon it will be for good. After we go to court that will be it. You'll be home with him forever."

Morgan reached for another slice of pizza and gave Justice a reassuring smile.

"When we go to court the judge will not grant any visitation rights to your mother. So it will be up to your dad if she can see you if she returns." Justice could tell talking about Monica bothered Morgan. She had to find some way to get Morgan to speak about her mother. She didn't want Morgan to get in court in front of the judge and fall apart.

"Morgan, I would like to share something with you. I completely understand you not wanting to talk about your mom. I know exactly what you—" Justice had to stop for a moment. She always got emotional when she discussed her own mother. "I know what you are going through. My mother died when I was only eight years old."

Morgan looked up at Justice with hurt in her eyes. Clearly she was shocked by what Justice had just said. "How did you deal with that?" she asked.

"My family. I had my aunt who loved me through it. But it was hard because not only did my mom die, I was a long way from home, in a whole different state where I knew no one. And where I was considered different because of the way I looked. But my aunt loved me, and she raised me to be proud, and now I'm OK. So I just want you to know I know how you feel, and you are not alone. Your dad loves you."

"I know he does, and I don't want to be anywhere else but with him. I miss my mom so much and pray every day that she is OK, and that she is safe. But if she were to come home tomorrow, I wouldn't want to go with her. I can't stand to move into another house and live like we are normal for six months or a year. And then have her wake up and decide we need to move again or she takes off for months until she is ready to come back. Justice, I just can't do it anymore." Morgan looked drained.

"OK, sweetheart, I get it." Justice reached across the table and grabbed Morgan's hands to comfort her. Justice felt her heart break for Morgan and all the pain she was going through at such a young age. There was no need to discuss anything further. Justice herself was past emotional.

"Whew," Justice said and wiped off the tears that had started to stream down her face. "Let's go ahead and eat this pizza before it gets cold."

"I agree," Morgan said and dug back into the pizza tray.

After finishing a couple more slices of pizza, Justice had the waitress wrap the rest up and put it in a carryout box for Morgan to take home. On the ride home they made small talk about things that Morgan had going on at school. Morgan realized that she enjoyed talking to Justice, and she felt bad for the way she had behaved the first couple of times they met.

Justice could see Austin had arrived home just as she expected. She pulled into the driveway and prepared to get out with Morgan.

Morgan gathered her things, but turned to Justice before opening the door. "Justice, I would like to really apologize for the way I acted all those other times before."

"You already apologized, remember?"

"No, I would like to really apologize from the bottom of my heart. The other time I just said what my dad ordered me to." Morgan gave her an apologetic smile. "But I am sorry, and I don't normally behave that way."

"Apology accepted," Justice smiled. "Now let's get you inside. I'll carry the pizza." Morgan handed Justice the pizza that had been sitting on her lap since they left the restaurant. They walked up to the door, and Morgan rang the doorbell.

"I lost my key, and Dad is supposed to be getting me another one made. I wish he would hurry up," Morgan said matter-of-factly.

Austin opened the door on the second ring. "Sorry it took me so long. I was upstairs."

"Hi, Dad." Morgan walked in and gave him a kiss on the cheek.

"I see you two made it back." Austin smiled looking at Justice.

"Yes," Justice smiled back. "Here." She handed him the pizza box.

"Sal's." Austin looked at the box. "Thanks. I love Sal's Pizzeria. He's the only one in town with real pizza sauce."

"And it's pepperoni, Dad. Can you believe that pepperoni is Justice's favorite too?" Morgan smiled.

"Wow," was Austin's only reply. No matter how he tried to get away from it, there was no escaping it. They were compatible in every way.

"I really enjoyed myself, Justice. But I have homework, so I'll see you later."

"I enjoyed you too," Justice laughed.

"Put this on the kitchen counter for me." Austin handed Morgan the pizza. "Justice, please excuse me, I forgot to invite you in."

"That's OK. I need to get going anyway. I just wanted to make sure Morgan got in safely."

"Well, let me walk you to your car." Austin closed the door behind him as he walked out into the night. All the streetlights were on. "I see you are still in two pieces, so I guess it went fine," Austin joked.

"Everything was great. I really enjoyed her. We talked, and I think she's ready."

"You think so?"

"Yeah, she'll be fine. You have done a wonderful job with her. She really loves and respects you."

"Thanks. She's my baby girl," Austin smiled proudly.

"Well, I will let you know soon what date we set for court. All you will need to do is show up with Morgan on that date. If I need anything before then, I will let you know."

"I guess we're getting close to the end. Before long I won't get to see you anymore."

"That's normally how it works after a case is over."

"Humph. I don't know if I will be able to do that. Justice, has anyone ever told you that you are stunning?"

Not wanting to go there Justice decided to put a stop to it. "Look, Austin, we can—" Austin cut her off. And before she knew it he reached out and gently pulled her into his body very closely and kissed her deeply. His tongue explored her mouth, and hers his, and without any control of her own Justice let out a moan. Her body awakened in spots where it had been asleep for a long time. And all too soon the kiss was over. Justice felt her balance almost break, and in that moment, she felt weak. Her immediate thought was to rip off Austin's shirt to expose his hardened dark chocolate six-pack chest and take him right there in the driveway. But slowly she regained her composure. And without so much as a good-bye, she got in her vehicle and turned on the ignition. She drove eighty all the way home where she immediately jumped in a cold shower.

Chapter Thirteen

"How was your vacation?"

"Hmmm . . ." was Candice's reply with a relaxing smile on her face. "It was good to just relax and play." Candice put a seductive smile on her face.

"And I guess Brian didn't have anything to do with that smile on your face, huh?"

"I guess you can say he did his part," Candice grinned. "Girl, I am just glad I took him along. I can't wait to do it again."

"Well, I'm glad you enjoyed yourself. And I'm also glad you're back."

"When are you going to take some time off? Because you need it. And more importantly, you need to get a man."

"Candice, let's not go there. It's way too early."

"Oh, and why didn't you tell me you were leaving? I heard about the job in New York. I was really hurt I had to hear it from another paralegal." Candice pouted her lips as if she was upset.

"So what was I suppose to do? Call you in Brazil to tell you? There was no way I was interrupting your time away. I left specific directions with Tabitha to not bother you with any calls. And that included myself. I wanted you to enjoy yourself."

"Justice, you are always so thoughtful, but, girl, information like that you know I want to know right away. Congratulations! I am so happy for you."

"Thanks," Justice said with no enthusiasm in her voice.

"Wait a minute, you don't seem happy at all. What's wrong?" Candice's smile changed to confusion.

"I don't know if I'm going to take it. I mean, I have already accepted it, but I'm having second thoughts."

"Why? This is your dream. This is why you've exhausted yourself and cut off contact with the outside world. So please enlighten me."

"It's my aunt Mattie. She's been sick, and I'm just worried about her. Of course, she wants me to go." Justice stood up and walked over to the window in her office.

"I'm sorry to hear about your aunt. What are you going to do? Because this is like a huge opportunity for you."

"I know."

"Whatever you decide, I support you on it because I wouldn't mind working for you for another twenty years," Candice joked.

"I'm sure you wouldn't," Justice smiled. "So what did you find on your investigation of Monica Jones?"

"She is quite the woman to research. But surprisingly, her life has been like some sort of a secret. I couldn't locate much of her family. And the ones that I could locate never have any contact with her."

"Humph," Justice replied.

"So basically, my investigation is done."

"Then we will proceed with full custody. After all, it is not our job to hunt anyone down but only to provide a measure of information to enlighten them of the seriousness of the situation."

"How soon would you like me to set the date? Here are all the papers of my findings, etc."

"Let's go with two weeks. Call down to the courthouse and set the date. Have Tabitha e-mail it to my agenda. In the meantime, I will contact our client and let him know to prepare for court."

"Speaking of the client, I heard he was the *quite* the cutie."

"Yeah? What else did Tabitha tell you?"

"Nothing, unless you mean the fact that he has eyes for you," Candice laughed.

"I *knew* she would say that. Actually, he is just quite the gentleman."

"Justice, please do not give me that. When are you going to allow yourself some happiness? You need to relax and let go. Go on a vacation to the Bahamas and take a cutie with you like him. I mean, if he is really cute, because I haven't had the chance to see him for myself," Candice joked.

Justice quickly clarified, "Trust me, he is handsome and a cutie. But he also is my client, so that means off limits."

"I don't care if he is Obama. If you like him, try him."

"Candice, get out of this office. I don't know what I'm going to do with you." Justice laughed at her bluntness. She knows Candice always tells it like it is, and she will give it to you straight with no chaser.

"I need to get going anyway. I have lunch with Brian." Candice smiled as she left the office.

"Tell him I said hi."

"Will do." Candice closed the door behind her.

Justice sat back down in her seat. Monica was still just as much a mystery to her as she was the day Austin had walked into her office. Candice was the best at finding out information about people and where they were. They joked all the time about how she should be a private investigator instead of a paralegal. Yet, she couldn't find any information on Monica. So the only information Justice had about her was what Austin had told her. She would have liked to have known more about the mysterious woman who, from time to time, left her beautiful daughter for months at a time to go off into the world. But for now, she would have to settle with what she did know and move forward with the proceedings. She would have to let Austin know that court would be in two weeks and to prepare for full custody of his daughter, Morgan. They would both be really happy. The ringing of the telephone interrupted Justice's thoughts. She slowly picked up the office telephone.

"Hello."

"What took you so long to say hello? Please tell me you are not daydreaming. Because that is not the day and the life of a successful judge," Kiki babbled playfully on the other end of the telephone.

"Kiki, what do you want?" Justice pretended to be annoyed.

"I was calling to see how you were doing. How are the headaches?" At that moment Justice knew Kiki was up to something.

"OK, give it up Something is going on. Now, tell me, because I know you did not call me to discuss my everlasting migraine headaches. So spit it out."

"Ha-ha, you think you know me so well. OK, OK, I have to tell you about my date with Clay."

"I already know you hated it," Justice cut in.

"Hated it? Justice, I loved it. I have never met or dreamed of going on a date with such a gentleman. Justice, he is so kind and thoughtful. He opened doors for me, he took his time when talking to me, and he don't abuse profanity. The first date went so well that we went out again right away."

"Wow, Kiki, I'm shocked." Justice was happy for her. "I wondered why I had not heard from you."

"I'm sorry, I didn't mean to disappear. I just been busy."

"Kiki, you don't have to apologize. I'm only kidding. You deserve this. I am just happy that you are happy. So when are you guys going out again?"

"Tonight. Clay wants to take me out to eat crabs. You know I ain't never tried that stuff, but for him, what the heck," Kiki giggled. "I eat way too much fried chicken anyway. Oh, and I invited him to the family reunion. He said he would love to meet my family."

Justice could hear all the enthusiasm in Kiki's voice. If she didn't know any better she would think that Kiki was a woman already in love.

"By the way, Aunt Sylvia called and said everything is taken care of. She finished the last of the arrangements so Aunt Mattie wouldn't have to worry about it."

"When does everyone from out of town start to arrive?" Justice inquired.

"I think Thursday and Friday, but most of the hotel reservations have been set up for Friday."

"Did anyone want to stay with me? They know I have all this space over here."

"No one said anything to me," Kiki smacked on gum.

"OK. Well, I guess that's it. Are the shirts going to be at Aunt Mattie's house?" Justice asked.

"That's what I needed to tell you. I knew there was something else. Aunt Sylvia said the shirts still need to be picked up. They have been paid for, but they won't be ready until Friday," Kiki filled her in.

"I can pick them up," Justice volunteered. "It's the least I can do."

Justice could hear the beep that came over the phone, and she knew it wasn't her phone. She could hear Kiki moving her phone around. She was probably trying to see who was chiming in on her phone.

With a schoolgirl giggle in her voice, Kiki said she had to go. "Girl, that's Clay on the other end. I'll talk to you later." Kiki ended the call before Justice could say good-bye.

Justice just smiled and put the phone back on its cradle. She remembered when she had those feelings for Keith. She missed that; she didn't miss Keith, just those times when it just felt good being in love.

Chapter Fourteen

"Hey, I was surprised to get your call. Come on in," Austin said as he stepped aside so that Justice could enter his house.

"Sorry to come on such short notice. I had planned to have Tabitha call you, but at the last minute she got ill so I sent her home," Justice explained.

"That's OK. It's not like I had anything planned," Austin assured her. "Come on in to the den and have a seat. I'm sure you remember the way." Austin pointed toward the den giving Justice the privilege to lead.

She walked there with Austin in tow. She wondered where Morgan was. The house seemed so quiet, as if no was home. But the closer Justice got to the den she could hear the television. She could also tell what was on by the narration of the voice. Austin was, without a doubt, watching *The First 48* on A&E. That channel was one of Justice's favorite channels to watch. She could sit and watch it for hours without ever getting bored. She found it ironic that Austin would be watching the same channel. But with him being a lead homicide detective, she wasn't shocked. Maybe it was where he got his ideas. With a chuckle in her mind she quickly dismissed that thought.

"Hey, Justice," Morgan said as she looked up from a book that she had been reading.

"Hey, Morgan. You reading?" Justice asked.

"Yeah, this is a hobby for me."

"Good, a little extra reading always helps. I hate to interrupt you, though."

"Oh, it's OK. I'm done now," Morgan assured her as she closed her book.

Austin entered the den and took a seat at the opposite end of the sectional from Justice. Morgan, who had her legs crossed Indian-style, held the book in her lap.

"Should I leave you two alone so that you can discuss business?" Morgan asked.

"Actually, no." Justice looked at both of them. "This concerns both of you."

Austin looked at Justice, giving her his undivided attention.

"The court date has been set for two weeks, Thursday after next at 2:00 P.M."

"So soon?" Morgan asked nervously.

"Morgan, honey, Justice has to speed this type of thing up. There's no need to drag it out," Austin explained, then looked at Justice.

"Did your paralegal find out anything? Any information about where she might be or anything?" Austin questioned.

"No, not a thing. Slate is as clean as a board," Justice confirmed.

"That's the way she wants it. You won't find her. She'll come back when she's ready," Morgan said. Justice and Austin both looked at her but didn't respond.

"Well, Justice," Austin said, "two weeks is right around the corner so we'll prepare."

"Morgan, are you ready to go in front of the judge?" Justice asked.

"Yes, I am." Morgan answered with a smile. "Besides, I need something exciting to do since school is out."

Justice had a shocked look on her face. "I forgot that school is out for the summer. Are you happy? Shouldn't you be outside riding bikes with your friends?" she asked.

Morgan let her head hang as if she were sad. "All of my friends are out of town. So the most fun I will have this summer will be jumping double Dutch at the YMCA." Morgan looked close to tears with that statement.

Justice noticed Morgan's sadness. "What about your dad? I'm sure he'll make sure you have big fun this summer on his days off," Justice tried to cushion her sadness.

"I sure am going to try," Austin chimed in. "I already told her I'm trying to be off around July for at least a full weekend. Then we can fly out somewhere."

Even with Austin's promise Morgan didn't seem hopeful because she knew if something came up on the job, her dad would not be able to go. And July was way too far off. She needed immediate fun. Justice could see the loneliness and sadness written all over Morgan's twelve-year-old face. And before she could stop herself she was trying to fix it.

"Ummm . . ." Justice cleared her throat. "I know this is a bit unusual, but this weekend my family reunion is coming up. We have family coming from all over. How about you to come out and join us? How would you feel about that? Morgan, there will be plenty of girls your age," Justice smiled.

"No, it really sounds nice, but we wouldn't want to impose on your family," Austin turned her down.

Justice could see Morgan's eyes light up. She knew that Morgan wanted to go, but she also knew that Morgan wouldn't leave her dad alone.

"Austin, it really wouldn't be a problem, and it will give Morgan something fun to talk about when school starts back. It will give her long boring summer excitement," Justice joked.

"All right, we'll come if you are sure it's not a problem," Austin gave in.

"Thanks, Dad." Morgan jumped off the couch and gave him a huge hug around the neck. Then she sealed it with a kiss on the cheek. "And thank you, Justice, for inviting us. Whew, I can't wait." Morgan headed toward her room doing the happy dance.

Shocked at her happiness, Justice and Austin both looked at each other and smiled as they watched Morgan disappear down the hall.

"Well, you certainly made her happy. I haven't seen her that happy over anything in a very long time. Thanks, Justice. I really appreciate it." Austin was sincere with his thanks.

"I'm glad to see her smile. But don't worry, you'll have a ball too. If there's one thing my family is good for, that's having a good time when they all get together," Justice smiled. She thought about her family and all the fun they were sure to have. Their family reunions were always a big turnout. But again, she wasn't sure what she had just gotten herself into. Now she would have to answer a thousand questions about who Austin was. But at least she wouldn't be the only one there with a guy no one knew. Clay would be there with Kiki, so she hoped that would distract people from Austin. And since Austin was only her client, maybe that would make it easier . . . or so she hoped.

Chapter Fifteen

The day of the family reunion had finally arrived, and Mississippi, true to itself, had a heat wave going on. Even with her car air conditioner blowing as high as it could, Justice was fighting the urge to turn around and ditch the family reunion. If it was this hot in her car, the park would be sweltering.

As she pulled into the park the first thing she fixed her eyes on was the pavilion and the huge fans they had set up to bring in as much cool air as possible. Justice knew that she would spend much of her time under the pavilion. With hesitation she climbed out of the car ready to meet and greet all of her family. To no surprise the kids were running about the park playing football, getting wet in swim trunks and bathing suits, and playing all sorts of games. The heat did not faze them. Seeing them happy raised Justice's confidence that she too could fight the boiling heat and have a good time. Besides, there was no migraine headache in sight.

"Justice, how you doing, baby?" Justice's cousin Pattie came out of nowhere. Pattie lived in Greenville, Mississippi. She had been Justice's mother's second cousin. She was always happy to see Justice. She too studied law and had been a successful lawyer, but she had retired two years back at the ripe old age of sixty. When Justice had been in law school and first became a practicing attorney, she had given Justice much advice.

"Hi, Pattie." Justice reached out and gave her a huge hug.

"Girl, you look as good as ever. I just want to congratulate you on your job offer. Mattie told me all about it." Pattie grinned from ear to ear.

"Thanks," Justice said, not wanting to talk about that. And it seemed she had been saved when Kiki started yelling her name. Justice looked up to see Kiki waving her over to the pavilion.

"Pattie, it's nice seeing you, and I'm sure we'll get to talk later, but I need to see what Kiki wants," Justice said feeling relieved. She would definitely have to thank Kiki later.

"OK, baby, you go ahead." Pattie dismissed Justice without continuation.

Justice rushed off in Kiki's direction, not stopping until she reached the pavilion. "Thank you so much," Justice said as soon as she reached Kiki. "Pattie had me cornered with the congratulation thing going on."

"Well, you can get used to that because Aunt Mattie has been telling anyone who will listen."

"Shit," Justice mouthed. She didn't normally use that type of language. This shocked Kiki.

"Could you repeat that?" Kiki laughed.

Justice looked at Kiki and laughed at her humor. She always knew how to make Justice smile.

"Look, just don't make clear eye contact with anybody and go tell Aunt Mattie right now to stop talking about it. But if you want my advice, be happy for yourself and embrace your success. You deserve it." Kiki shrugged her shoulders and turned to walk away.

"Wait," Justice called out to Kiki, "what did you want?"

"Huh?" Kiki seemed confused.

"You waved me over here. Why?"

"Nothing in particular," Kiki smiled. "I have to get back to Clay. I left him over there with Cousin Jeff, and you know he's given him the recipe to chitlins burgers."

The thought of that so-called recipe turned Justice's stomach. Their cousin Jeff was a very odd person who would feed you roadkill if you let him. The rule was never eat or taste *anything* Cousin Jeff had to offer. "Please hurry up and save him," Justice encouraged Kiki. Just as Kiki walked away Justice spotted Aunt Mattie over at a table stretching about a mile high with food. Justice immediately walked over to her.

"Hi, Auntie." Justice reached out and gave her aunt a hug.

"Hey, baby. What took you so long to get here? I thought I was gon' have to call you," Aunt Mattie fussed with a smile.

"All this heat, Auntie. I just couldn't get a move on knowing how hot it was out here," Justice confessed.

"I know, but, baby, you only get to see yo' familee gather like this once every couple of years. It's important that you come out and fellowship wit' yo' familee."

"I know, Auntie, and that's why I'm here," Justice agreed. "Is there anything I can do to help?"

"Naw, everythang is already done. Yo' aunt Sylvia took care of everythang. She made sure I didn't have to lift a finger. Bless her heart," Aunt Mattie smiled.

Justice looked up at her auntie's face, and this time she thought her aunt looked a little pale and tired. This concerned her, and even though she didn't want to spoil her aunt from having a good time, but she had to ask.

"Auntie, are you feeling all right? I noticed you look a little tired."

"Justice, how many times I got to tell you I am fine. But I'm still trying to adjust to this new insulin Doctor Shapiro has me taking," Aunt Mattie admitted. "But I'm fine."

"OK, I just had to ask," Justice smiled. Catching a glimpse of Clay and Kiki playing around and laughing made Justice laugh. "Auntie, what do you think of Clay?" she asked.

"Chile, he is a nice young man. And I hope it works out because yo' cousin is in love." Aunt Mattie grinned as she too looked off into their direction. "I can't remember a time when she felt so secure and happy in a relationship. He's good for her."

"That he is," Justice agreed with Aunt Mattie.

"Well, I'ma go over here and have a seat in front of one of these here fans," Aunt Mattie said. "You are more than welcomed to join me." And without another word she headed toward the tables in the pavilion. Justice followed close behind her aunt, anxious to sit in front of the blowing fan. Just as she went to sit down she saw Austin approaching with Morgan in tow.

"Auntie, I'll be right back." Justice headed in their direction.

Austin could not impede the smile that crept across his face when he saw Justice coming toward him. Her hair was bouncing, and her skin was glowing, not to mention she had on thigh-high shorts that showed off her beautiful long legs. He contemplated reaching out and hugging her but decided it would be too much, not mention it might horrify Morgan, so he chilled.

"You guys made it," Justice said as she stopped directly in front of Austin.

"Sorry we're a little late, but I had a murder-suicide call at 1:00 this morning, so I didn't get any sleep until about 8:00 A.M. I woke up a little later than I intended."

"Austin, you should have stayed home." Justice felt guilty. "I would have understood."

"Stay home? No, you may have forgiven me, but *she* wouldn't." Austin smiled as he pointed to Morgan who was standing behind him looking around the park at all the things that were going on.

"It looks they are having so much fun." Morgan had fixed her gaze on the kids running through the water getting wet and screaming for more.

"Why don't you join them?" Justice suggested.

"No way, I didn't bring a bathing suit." Morgan smiled as she turned her attention to Justice. "I'm sorry. Hi, Justice," Morgan spoke realizing had not greeted Justice because she had been caught up in the action going on at the park.

"Hi, sweetheart," Justice smiled.

"Why don't I introduce you to some of the girls your age?" Justice offered. She could see the anxious look on Morgan's face.

"You don't have to do that. I'm not shy," Justice smiled. "Dad, is it OK?"

"Sure, honey, go ahead."

"Morgan, just one minute. I would like to introduce you to my aunt Mattie."

"OK."

Justice turned around and started back toward the pavilion with Austin and Morgan following her. Aunt Mattie had leaned back in her chair enjoying the air coming from the fan by the time Justice approached.

"Auntie," Justice said.

Mattie sat up in her chair when she heard Justice call her name.

"I have some people here I want you to meet. This here is Austin," Justice pointed.

"How are you ma'am?" Austin spoke first while reaching his hand out for a shake.

"I'm just fine. I'm pleased to meet you finally. I've heard some good things about you," Aunt Mattie replied returning Austin's handshake.

Justice shot a shocked glare at her aunt. She couldn't believe she had said that. Now Austin would know that she thought about him when he wasn't around. She quickly changed the subject. "Auntie, this is his beautiful daughter, Morgan."

"How you doing, baby?"

"Hi," Morgan spoke softly, following Austin's trend reaching for a handshake.

Aunt Mattie quickly dismissed her handshake. "Uh-uh, no handshake. You come right on over here and give yo' aunt Mattie a hug."

Justice wasn't shocked with her aunt's reaction to Morgan because she loved kids. But she was shocked at Morgan who, without hesitation, reached out and leaned down and gave Aunt Mattie a huge hug.

"You are beautiful, just like Justice say you are. Now from now on, you call me Aunt Mattie, OK?"

"Yes, ma'am," Morgan complied with a smile.

"Are you hungry?"

"No, I'm OK for now. I do want to go talk to those girls." Morgan nodded her head in the direction of some girls standing under a nearby tree.

"Those are my grandnieces over there. If it's all right with yo' dad you just gon' right ahead," Aunt Mattie nodded.

Morgan again looked at Austin who gave her an OK nod. Right away, she headed off in the direction of the girls.

"Austin, are you hungry, baby?" Aunt Mattie asked.

"I wouldn't mind eating," he said with a smile plastered on his face.

"Justice, take him over there and fix him a plate. It's plenty to eat. I don't want you leaving here on no empty stomach, ya hear? You are family," Aunt Mattie said, and Justice knew she meant every word.

"Yes, ma'am," Austin replied with a smile.

"Uh-uh, you call me Aunt Mattie too." She shook her head after giving Austin complete instructions.

Austin smiled again and nodded his head in agreement.

"Come on, Austin." Justice started walking toward the food tables that were overflowing with goodies. Once at the table Austin grabbed himself a plate and piled it with tasty-looking food. Then they headed toward an empty table where Kiki and Clay soon joined them.

"Hi, Kiki," Austin said when she approached the table.

"Austin, right?" Kiki asked with a smile.

"You got it," he smiled back.

"Hi, Clay," Justice spoke.

"Hey, Council," Clay said with a grin.

"So, Justice, you didn't tell me you had invited Austin." Kiki gave her a sly grin. Justice knew she would tease her.

"Really? I thought I did," Justice played along. "Kiki, I invited Austin and Morgan to the family reunion," she teased her back.

"Where is Morgan?" Kiki asked.

"She's over there." Justice pointed to Morgan who was now comfortably standing over by a tall, shady oak tree with a bunch of girls from Justice's family. Morgan seemed to be having a grand time. She was laughing and playing around. It warmed Justice's heart to see her fit right in.

Kiki smiled. "She seems to enjoying herself."

"Yeah," Austin replied. "All of her friends went out of town for the summer. She has been a little lonely, so I'm glad Justice invited us out."

"That was nice of her." Kiki smiled at Justice.

Justice kicked Kiki under the table. She was going to get her later.

"Austin, you look so familiar to me," Clay remarked.

"I was thinking the same thing when I saw you," Austin admitted.

"Where do you work?" Clay asked.

"I'm a homicide detective for Gulfport PD."

"Maybe that's how I know you." Clay seemed to rack his brain until he found the answer. "Did you work on that Donavan and Chaney murder?"

"Yep, that would be me and my partner, Trent."

"I knew it. I prosecuted that case. I remember that case so well. You two guys had heart. The victims' families spoke highly of you two detectives." The look on Clay's face showed his trip down memory lane.

"I remember that. My heart really went out to them. Had it not been for your determination they would have walked. We found the evidence, and you made it stick. Thanks, man," Austin said with sincerity in his tone.

"No problem. That's what I do, and with hardworking detectives like you, those are the results we get."

"OK, you two, enough of shop talk," Justice joked.

"I agree, Justice. Maybe we should play some sack races," Kiki suggested.

"I'm game." Justice stood up and flipped her hair out of her face.

"I mean, that is, if these guys don't mind getting beat by women," Kiki joked putting her game face on.

"Getting beat? Whoever said we would get beat?" Austin pushed his empty plate to the side and wiped his hands on a napkin.

"You must have read my mind. It's on." Clay reached over and gave Austin a pound fist to fist.

"Then follow us." Kiki grabbed Justice by the arm, and they headed toward the sack races laughing.

After going back and forth on the sack races four times with Justice and Kiki winning each time, the two men finally gave in. Joking around and laughing they were having way too much fun. Clay decided they should participate in the volleyball game that was going on across the park from them. Since some of Justice's cousins already had a game going men against women it was decided that they should join right in.

Twenty minutes into the game it was clear that Justice and Austin were both pros at volleyball. Both of their teams seem to cheer them on and depend on them to keep them in the lead. While waiting for the ball to be served over by Austin's team, Justice glanced over to see Morgan still laughing with some of her younger cousins, some of which she couldn't even remember their names. It made her happy to see Morgan enjoying herself. Justice smiled in Austin's direction and nodded for him to look at over at Morgan. He turned in time to see her still laughing. Moving his lips, Austin silently mouthed thank you to Justice. The day was turning out great. Justice hadn't imagined them having this much fun. In fact, she thought the day would be filled with the questions of inquiring minds about Austin. Instead, everyone was just enjoying themselves. Justice served the ball in full action, but was sure she had heard someone scream. Moving backward, falling into step to hit at the ball, she heard the scream again. But this time Kiki heard it as well because she turned toward the scream.

"That's Auntie Sylvia," Kiki mouthed and took off running toward the screaming which at this point was loud and clear.

Justice took off behind Kiki at full speed. At the same time it seemed everyone was running in the same direction. Justice had been running so fast that she didn't notice that she had bypassed Kiki. As she approached the pavilion she could see Aunt Sylvia standing over her aunt Mattie.

"What happened?" Justice yelled as she dropped to her knees kneeling over the elderly woman.

"I don't know. We were standing here talking, and she just fell backward. Thank God Kevin was standing behind her or she would have hit the concrete," Sylvia said nervously.

"Auntie, Auntie," Justice yelled. "Call 911. Please," Justice screamed to no one in particular while crying hysterically.

"Oh my God, what's wrong with her?" Kiki asked in hurried breaths when she finally reached Justice. "Justice, what's wrong?" Kiki continued to yell with a face dripping from instant tears.

"I don't know. Aunt Sylvia just said she passed out," Justice said through choked up tears. In the background, she could hear the sirens approach, and then people yelling, "Step back!" After that, everything became a blur.

ððð

Justice and Kiki had both ridden in the ambulance with Aunt Mattie while the paramedics worked to keep her stabilized. Horrified, they both watched with racing hearts as their aunt seemed to barely cling to life. As soon as they reached the emergency room everything happened quickly. People came out of nowhere to help assist the paramedics, and before long, Justice and Kiki were being forced out of the room into the waiting area.

The bright lights from the ceiling that seem to be beaming directly on Justice started to aggravate her. Kiki rushed over to her, and they hugged each other tight and cried.

"Are either of you related to the patient?" a voice came from behind them.

"Yes." Both Justice and Kiki turned and answered at the same time. The nurse gave them a confused look.

"She's our aunt," Justice answered as calmly as she could muster, then cleared her throat.

"Oh, I see." The nurse gave them a sympathetic smile. "Well, we have some papers that need to be filled out concerning your aunt's health and insurance information. So if you could please follow me." The nurse with her short hair that seemed to fit her head like a cap waddled all the way back to her desk with Justice and Kiki hot on her heels.

"I need you to fill out all of these." She handed Justice the forms. "You can have a seat over there, and I'll come over to get them."

"But when will the doctor come out to let us know what's going on with our aunt?" Kiki asked with attitude.

"As soon as they get her stabilized the doctor will come out." The nurse remained calm. "And as soon you fill out those papers we can notify her doctor."

"If all you need is her doctor's name we can tell you that. But fuck filling out these forms." Kiki had tears traveling down her face. At that point Justice knew she had to get Kiki under control.

"Kiki, Kik." Justice grabbed her by the arm and pulled her off to the side. "Now you have to calm down. That nurse is only doing her job, and we need to be strong for Aunt Mattie, OK?"

Kiki nodded letting Justice know that she agreed. "Let's just have a seat right over there." Justice pointed to the empty seats by a huge window overlooking the parking lot. Before too long the nurse came over to retrieve the forms from Justice.

"Justice, what if she's not OK? She's all way we have." Kiki sucked in her breath to keep from crying.

"Don't say that. She's going to be fine. Let's pray. Let's maintain what Auntie has always instilled in us, faith." Justice grabbed Kiki by the hand and said a quick prayer.

Just as she wrapped up the prayer all the family from the reunion started to arrive in droves. Aunt Sylvia came over and hugged them both. "Has the doctor come out yet?"

"No, we are still waiting," Kiki answered.

"This is my fault," Justice said remorsefully. "I should have made her go to the emergency room. I knew something was wrong with her." Everyone started to look at her. "Her face was all pale, but she said she was fine. But it's my fault because I should have known better."

"Justice, baby, there is no way this is your fault. It's nobody's fault and don't let me hear you say that again," Aunt Sylvia said in a matter-of-fact tone.

Kiki looked up to see Clay turn the corner. She immediately got out of her seat and ran to him. Clay embraced her, telling her it would be OK. Justice's heart swelled from the peace she saw on Kiki's face when she caught sight of Clay. Justice started to sit back in her seat when around the same corner Clay had appeared from came Austin followed by Morgan. Justice was shocked that Austin had come all the way to the hospital to check on her aunt who he had only met a couple of hours ago. Slowly she got out of her seat and moved toward him.

"How is she?" Austin seemed to look right through to Justice's soul.

"We don't know yet," Justice said trying to control the tremor that was threatening her voice. But unable to control herself she fell directly into Austin's waiting arms. Austin held on to Justice for dear life. At that very moment he wished he could do something—anything—to take away all her fears. He wanted to know that her auntie would be OK.

Justice was so wrapped up in Austin's protection that she didn't want to let go. As she tried to recover herself she got a look at Morgan who looked as if she too had been crying. "Morgan, sweetheart, are you, OK?" Justice went to her and gave her a huge hug which Morgan kindly returned.

"I'm OK," Morgan sniffed. "I'm so sorry, Justice." Morgan began to cry all over again.

"No, baby, you don't have to be sorry. I'm OK, see? My eyes are all dry." Justice gave Morgan a hopeful smile.

"I know I just met Aunt Mattie, but I think I loved her right away. I want to get to know her." Morgan tried to control her trembling voice.

"Honey, you will because she loves you too, OK?"

Morgan nodded her head.

A voice announced, "I need to speak to the immediate family of Mattie Jones."

"We are her immediate family," Justice pointed between herself and Kiki.

"Hi, I'm Dr. Chaz. I will be filling in until Dr. Shapiro arrives. Ms. Jones seems to have had a reaction to the new insulin she has been taking. Basically, her blood levels dropped way below normal. But we now have them under control."

"Oh, thank God," Justice sighed with relief.

"When can we see her?" Kiki asked.

"Soon. Dr. Shapiro will be here any minute now. He will prescribe a different insulin, and she should be ready to go home in the morning. So just have a seat and I'll send a nurse out to get you as soon all is situated."

"Thank you so much, Dr. Chaz." Justice thanked him and shook his hand.

"Whew," Kiki said. "I was so afraid."

Kiki and Justice hugged each other again. "Faith, remember," Justice said.

"Just like Auntie taught us," Kiki smiled.

Everyone sat out in the waiting area for a while until the nurse said it was OK for some of the adults to go in to see Aunt Mattie. After seeing her, everyone started to feel better that she had awakened and regained her strength so they started to leave. Dr. Shapiro had arrived and confirmed that she would be released first thing in the morning. Aunt Sylvia had decided that she would stay so that Justice and Kiki could take care of the cleanup at the park.

 working as ∂∂∂

"Justice, how did the cleanup go?" Aunt Mattie yelled from the living room. She had just been released from the hospital a couple of hours earlier. Kiki had to go to work so Justice had come over to help take care of her. Dr. Shapiro had changed her insulin and otherwise gave her a clean bill of health. The incident had given the whole family quite a scare. But Dr. Shapiro assured them that everything else looked fine. Her lupus was responding well to the medication; her blood pressure was under control. The only thing they needed to get on board was her diabetes, and the new insulin should do the trick. Justice came of the kitchen with a piping hot cup of tea.

"It went great. Everyone pitched in, including Clay, Morgan, and Austin. With all that help it was done in no time."

"Good. I was worried. Without me or Sylvia there, I'm surprise it didn't go awry." Aunt Mattie gave a chuckle. "But I'm proud of all of you."

"Auntie, you worry too much. You have got to let us take the reins sometimes. We can handle it. You made sure of that. If you didn't teach me and Kiki nothing else, you taught us to be independent and strong," Justice assured her. "When my mother sent me to you, she knew exactly what she was doing. I love you, Auntie," Justice reminded her.

"I know, baby, and I love you too." Aunt Mattie sipped her tea that she was stirring. "Now this little episode doesn't change a thing. You are still moving to New York. I'm fine. Dr. Shapiro confirmed that."

Justice looked at her aunt and smiled. She knew she wouldn't let up on Justice going to New York no matter what. Justice wanted to go to New York. There was no denying that, but she also wanted to stay. For her, it wasn't in stone yet, but she knew staying would probably spike her aunt's health with disappointment.

"Aunt Mattie, I want to ask you something that I never asked you before."

Mattie could tell this was serious because of the heartrending look on Justice's face.

"What can you tell me about my dad? What happened to him?"

Justice could tell by the look on her aunt's face that she was unprepared for that question.

"I mean, I know he was killed, but that's it. And the only reason I know that is because I overheard my mom talking to one of her friends when I was six. But I would like to know about it. Like how did he meet my mom?"

Aunt Mattie shifted her body in her seat. "I'll tell you, baby, 'cause you are a grown woman and you have the right to know." She took a sip of her tea and cleared her throat. "Your mother was always such a beautiful child. Special in her own way. I remember when my sister, your grandmother, used to bring her down here. She would be the star of the show. She just had this huge presence about her. Just like you." Aunt Mattie smiled with the thought in her head.

"She never did anything to upset your grandmother; she was always responsible. Your grandmother was always so proud of her. She felt like maybe she was the perfect daughter. That is, until she came home with your father, a well-bred Latino." Aunt Mattie started laughing. "Chile, your grandmother nearly died. I will never forget she called me crying on the phone. I told her to get over it and that I would pray for her."

"But wait, Auntie, wasn't my grandfather white?" Justice was confused.

"As the clouds in the sky but your grandmother got in her head that Latinos were different. She prayed every night that your mother would have a change of heart. But that never happened. In fact, your mother and father got closer, and eventually your grandmother grew to love him. They even all came to visit me in Gulfport once, but that's before you were born. And boy, was he handsome." Auntie smiled, but then it faded as quickly as it had come. Justice could tell she was thinking something awful.

"Now, I'ma tell you this part the way I got it. You had just been born, that I know for sure; you had been in this world for all of six months. And they both loved you so much. You were their pride and joy. Happiness was theirs. They had just gotten engaged and everything was going good. Well, one night your dad was on his way home from work on the subway. Apparently some guys approached him and demanded his wallet. They say he wouldn't give it up, so one of the guys stabbed him in the chest twice. But your dad was not dead and started to fight back. That's when the other one got scared because your dad was choking the one that had stabbed him. So he grabbed your dad from the back, and he threw him onto the train tracks." Tears flooded Justice's face as she sat and listened to the story of how her father was murdered, all for a lousy few bucks.

"Both boys were just a few years younger than your father because he was only twenty-four years old. They both got life sentences. Your mother was devastated, but she decided not to let you down."

"I just hate that I didn't get to know him," Justice cried. "You know I just wish he was here to give me advice. I wish she was here also. Sometimes I just feel empty without them, Auntie."

"Ah, baby, it's OK. You get it all out. You have a right to be upset. But God has his plan, you know that. I raised you to know that. You keep pushin' the way you pushin'. They are both smilin' down on you. They both know your accomplishments, and they haven't missed out on you."

Justice loved her aunt so much. She was always there for her. "Thank you, Auntie, for raising me and loving me. I couldn't have asked for a better person to be here for me."

"Who said I was through raisin' you? I still got some things to do," Aunt Mattie grinned. "But I am so glad you didn't have to leave for New York before the reunion. I saw you having all that fun. I know you and Kiki really enjoyed yourself."

"We did, even though it was smoking hot it was fun," Justice agreed.

"And I tell you, that Austin is a hunk," Aunt Mattie blurted out.

"Auntie!" Justice had a shocked grin on her face.

"What? Chile, he is. Back in my day, I would be trying to snatch him up real quick," she said matter-of-factly. "Uh-huh, sho' would," Aunt Mattie sealed.

"Auntie, I can't believe you said that," Justice laughed.

"Honey, it's the truth. That man is handsome, and he a gentleman. You need to snatch him up like yesterday's business. Don't let that good thing pass you by."

"I can't do that."

"Justice, baby, he got it bad for you. It's written all over his face and yours too. I watched you two together yesterday, and it was plain as day."

"Auntie, I have to object to that. Yesterday we were two people playing games and having fun. That's it." Justice rested her case.

"Objection denied in my courtroom. Your aunt has been living too long not to know love when she sees it. And this is it." She pointed her finger. "You see, I always had doubts about Keith."

Justice looked up at her aunt. "Why didn't you say something?"

"I wanted to, but you had that look in your eyes. You were in love, and I thought maybe it would be OK. But something about him just always made me think twice. I mean, I knew he was nice guy, but I just never thought he was for you. But, Justice, God know his plan, and he moved Keith out your life for a reason. I know how much you loved him, but God knows best. And I'm telling you, Austin, that is yo' husband, baby." Aunt Mattie had became emotional, and a single tear slid down her right cheek. "And that Morgan, ain't she just a beautiful creature?" Aunt Mattie chuckled.

"Yeah, she is," Justice agreed with a smile plastered on her face.

"She likes you too, Justice. A beautiful family is what you all will make one day."

"Auntie, I think you are forgetting one thing."

"Yeah, what's that?" She sipped her tea never taking her eyes off Justice.

"New York."

Aunt Mattie took a few more sips of her tea all the while considering what Justice had just said. "Let me tell you something. And this you may already know. Love conquers all, and when I say love, I don't mean passion. I mean true love, and nothing can't stand in the way of that. It may be a challenge, don't get me wrong. But it can't stand in the way for long because love will remain in the driver's seat. You remember that." Aunt Mattie, Counsel-at-large, had spoken her piece.

Chapter Sixteen

Austin pulled into Ocean Springs gated community anxious to find Justice's house after he had been cleared by security to enter. She had invited him over to discuss some last and final details of the case. He hadn't seen her since he had helped out with the cleanup after the family reunion, and it had felt like a lifetime. And although he was ready to go to court to gain full custody of Morgan, he had started to dread what that would mean after. No more Justice. Austin pulled in front of the address that was on the GPS system where the directions had led him straight to her house. His first thought was there was no way she lived there alone. It was a huge mansion, especially for one person. There was a running waterfall lit up out front. When Austin pulled in, he had to drive around a circular driveway in order to reach the front door. There was a three-car garage outside that didn't reveal any of Justice's vehicles.

Austin climbed out of his truck and walked up to the double doors that led into the entryway and rang the doorbell.

Justice swung the door open with a smile plastered on her face. "I see you found your way. I thought maybe you had gotten lost."

"No, my GPS led me straight here," Austin smiled. "Your mansion was right on my radar," he joked.

"This is not a mansion," Justice laughed. "Come on in." She stepped back so he could enter.

When Austin stepped into the foyer he was totally amazed. To the right of the foyer entry was a circular staircase that led upstairs. And right there in the foyer was a real crystal chandler hanging from the high ceiling. "Wow, Justice, this is beautiful. Are you sure you live here alone?" Austin continued to joke. He thought the house was huge.

"Yes, I'm sure," Justice smiled. Everyone that visited her for the first time had asked her the same question. They couldn't believe she lived alone. But she loved the space. She wouldn't trade it for anything. "That's the reason for the top-notch security. Believe it or not, as much as I wanted this house when I moved in I was afraid," she revealed.

"Why afraid? I know this community is fairly new, about maybe seven years. And nothing remotely bad has ever been reported."

"Well, that is, if you exclude that senator who beat his wife," Justice reminded him.

"Oh yeah, I forgot about that. But other than that you are safe." Austin gave her a reassuring smile.

Justice smiled back and gave him a slight nudge on the shoulder. "You are funny. Follow me." Justice She led him into her entertainment room. The artwork throughout the room was phenomenal. Austin loved it, and it was clear her style was Italian. She had wine chilling on ice. "Did you find my Aunt Sylvia's house easily?" Justice asked him.

"It was actually quite close to my house. Not to mention Tammy was standing on the curb waiting for us when we arrived. I tell you, those two have been nonstop on the phone chatter bugs since they met at the reunion," Austin laughed.

"I know, my aunt told me."

"I don't think Morgan is that close to her friends that she goes to school with," Austin admitted.

"Really?" Justice seemed shocked. "Well, I'm glad she enjoyed the reunion and that she found her best friend at the same time."

They both laughed.

"Yeah, it's amazing what you can find at random reunions. Especially when it's been right up under you, not far away all along," Austin said staring at Justice.

Justice read directly through his hint lines, and she knew he was definitely talking about her without a doubt. And to be honest, she didn't feel like denying it. But she also wanted to get to the point of inviting him over.

"Um, are you ready to eat? I took the liberty of ordering takeout from your favorite Hunan House."

Austin smiled, and Justice knew she had made the right decision.

"We can eat right in here and talk. I can pour you some wine, but I also have water and soda in the fridge."

"Wine will do just fine."

While enjoying their Chinese dishes and discussing things about the case Justice and Austin continued to sip wine. She couldn't keep her eyes off his lips that moved so sweetly that, for the life of her, she couldn't the get urge to kiss them out of her head.

"So what's your story?" Austin could no longer resist the urge to ask.

"Really, you don't want to know that story. It could take all night." Justice refilled her wineglass.

"Good thing I have all night then." He took another sip of his wine.

"Austin, why would you like to know that?"

"It's not the story I just want to know about you. Who is Justice, if I may ask?"

"Justice is a black mixed with Latino female from New York. That should say it all. It should explain the green eyes, skin tone, and the hair." She bounced her hair with a flip of her hand. "A little perm and the hair went from curly to straight. And the only way to explain the green eyes since I'm Latino is my grandparents. My mother's father was white."

Austin thought he saw hurt in Justice's eyes by the time she was done releasing her explanation of her identity. "Are you OK? I didn't mean to pry about what your race was," Austin said with sincerity in his voice. He felt bad. He hadn't meant to make her think he was like the others who had questioned who or what she was. "I just thought you could tell me about your background."

"I'm sorry, you didn't deserve that," she apologized. "It's just when some people here meet me, that seems to be their only concern. They are always trying to figure me out because of my looks. It can be hurtful."

"I am sorry. That is not what I was trying to imply at all." Austin wanted to be clear.

"I know you weren't." Justice seat her wineglass down. "I moved here when I was eight. I was only supposed to be here until my mom returned from the military. But she was killed before she could return. My dad was killed when I was a baby, so with no one left in New York to care for me, I stayed here with Auntie Mattie. Of course, I had other family members there, but no one my mother entrusted me with. That's how I ended up here in the first place."

"See? That was interesting."

"Wait, that's not my entire story," Justice informed him.

"I'm all ears."

"My mother always wanted to be a lawyer. I mean, I can remember being four years old and her telling me all about the law. It was her true passion. That was her whole reason for joining the military. She knew that they would pay for her to attend college. Anyhow, after she died I decided that I would make her dream come alive. After all, I had to live up to my name, Justice."

Justice paused and gave Austin a smile which he returned. "Now, once I entered college, I knew that law was truly my passion as well as my future so I explored and had fun doing it. That's when I entered law school and meet the man of my dreams, Keith. Now, in my mind, Keith would become my husband. We were compatible and after passing the bar, we both got into first-class firms here in Mississippi. Things couldn't get any better for us, but our success had just begun. We were both taking on high-profile cases and winning. Success was truly ours, and then came the promotions to partner at the firms for both of us. And that's when he decided to pop the question: marriage. Of course I accepted. Why wouldn't I? He was the perfect man, but he turned out to be not so perfect when I discovered, via the newspaper, that he was going to marry someone else. So that was the end of the perfect life, and that concludes my story." Justice picked up her wineglass and took a big swig trying to avoid Austin staring eyes.

Before Justice could protest, Austin had taken the empty wineglass out of her hand and pulled her into him. Without any hesitation, he kissed her passionately, his tongue penetrating her mouth, giving her the most passionate kiss she had ever received. But Justice didn't hold back; she met his kiss stroke by stroke. Forgetting that entire attorney-client business, she straddled Austin and wrapped her arms tightly around his neck. She could feel him growing under her and wanted him as much as he wanted her. Austin began to explore Justice's hard nipples which he felt brushing up against his chest. His lips found her neck, and he kissed her neck softly as she threw her head back and rocked on his hardened manhood that continued to grow by the second. Not being able to take any more, Austin pulled Justice's shirt up and admired her nipples as he hungrily took them one by one into his warm, waiting mouth. Justice moaned out loud without shame. She couldn't take any more either. he had to have him inside her. She lifted her body forward and whispered in his ear.

"Let's take this to my room. I have protection in there."

Austin answered her by pulling her back in for a deep kiss. Then he picked her up while she still straddled him and walked up the circular staircase leading to Justice's waiting bedroom where they shared and explored and devoured each other for hours.

Chapter Seventeen

Justice had been sitting at her desk all day dreaming, and Austin was high priority on her mind. She didn't know what to feel about the passionate night they had spent together. Secretly, she kicked herself for letting it go that far. But deep down, her feelings for him were swarming, not to mention she had released a ton of stress she didn't even know she had. Her migraines had all but disappeared. There had not been one sign of a migraine since the night they had shared.

On the other hand, what was she doing? Attorneys didn't sleep with their clients, especially when they have plans to move away, far away. She had decided to take the job in New York. Since Dr. Shapiro had changed Aunt Mattie's insulin, she had been doing great. She was up and about, her blood pressure was good, and she was back out in her garden. Things for her couldn't be better so Justice only had a short time left in Gulfport.

Buzz, buzz the office phone sang.

"Justice, Kiki is here," Tabitha informed her.

"Send her in," Justice replied. She wondered what Kiki could want this time of day. Normally she would be at work.

"What's up?" Kiki strutted into her office wearing with the biggest smile Justice had seen on her in a long time. As a matter of fact, it wasn't just a smile. Justice was sure she had won the lottery. Even her clothes were happy.

"What brings you by this time of day? Don't tell me— I know. They promoted you to front-end manager, right?"

"Guess again," Kiki smiled.

"You hit the lottery," Justice smiled with uncertainty.

"Wrong again. And I thought you knew me so well. But . . . how about *this*?" Kiki held up her left hand and flashed a ring that blinded Justice. "He proposed! Clay proposed!"

"You're getting married?" Justice's mouth flew open. "OH MY GOD, YOU'RE GETTING MARRIED. AGGGH!" Justice screamed as she jumped out of her seat and ran around her desk and wrapped her arms around Kiki. They hugged each other tight jumping up and down.

"What is going on in here?" Tabitha burst in her eyes bulging with wonder.

"Tabitha, Kiki is getting married." Justice spilled with pure excitement.

"Congratulations, Kiki." Tabitha walked over for an embrace.

"Thank you." Kiki held up her hand in her own face again to admire the ring. "I can't believe it. I am getting married. I never thought I would get to say those words." Tears start to trickle down her face.

"I always knew you would." Justice hugged her again. "So have you told Auntie yet?"

"Actually, no. I had planned to go by the house when I leave here. I had to tell my best friend first." Kiki looked at Justice teary-eyed. "You my cousin."

Tears started sliding down Justice's face now. She couldn't hold it anymore. It warmed her heart to know that Kiki thought of her more than just a cousin. They were in every way that mattered best friends. "So when is the wedding?" Justice asked after reaching for a Kleenex for her and Kiki.

"Congratulations, again, Kiki," Tabitha said, then excused herself. She had to get back to her desk. Justice and Kiki had forgotten she was still in the room.

"We are going to do it right away. Clay said he does not want to wait. He wants me to become his wife as soon as possible. So I figured I could get everything planned and set up in the next couple of months, maybe around November."

Tears started to invade Justice again. "What's the matter?" Kiki asked.

"I was just thinking, I'm leaving for New York soon, which means I won't be able to help you plan the wedding. I always assumed I would be here to help you plan your special day," Justice pouted.

"That's OK. I forgive you as long as you don't miss the wedding." Kiki gave her an assuring smile. "Now *that* I can't forgive."

"I promise I won't miss it for the world. I will be here rain, sleet, or snow," Justice promised, meaning every word. There was no way she would miss Kiki's big day.

"Good, now that that is settled let's go tell Aunt Mattie," Kiki beamed.

"Sure. I don't have anything urgent." Justice picked up her phone to tell Tabitha to hold all her calls. She grabbed her purse, and they headed out. Aunt Mattie would be thrilled.

Chapter Eighteen

Austin pulled into Red Lobster and quickly found a parking space. He gave the lot a quick glance to see if he noticed either one of Justice's vehicles. Although he was aware that she had a third vehicle that he had not seen yet, he didn't see the Mercedes or the Range Rover so he was convinced he had arrived before her. He had texted her first thing that morning and asked her to meet him for lunch. All morning he had been feeling confident but on the drive over, his nerves started to get to him, but for him, it was now or never.

He would just lay his feelings right out on the line for her. Austin knew how Justice felt about a new relationship, but for him, it was worth a try. He had to let her know how he felt. They had not spoken since their last encounter, and he was eager see her.

After getting inside the restaurant he asked for a booth seating so they could have a little bit of privacy. No sooner had he sat down and ordered a soda then Justice arrived, and as always, she looked stunning.

"Hey," Justice spoke with a smile.

"Nice seeing you, again." Austin stood to greet her with a slight peck on the cheek.

"Sorry I'm running a little behind. I almost couldn't get out of the office. It was one thing after another. But I'm here." She settled into her seat comfortably.

"That's OK, I'm just glad you could make it." Austin couldn't take his eyes off of her. He was simply mesmerized by her natural beauty. Today, instead of the wrap, she had her hair pulled back into a soft ponytail that showed off all her pretty features. If she wanted he was sure she could hit the runway at that very moment. God, she was beautiful!

"So what's your favorite meal here?" Justice asked as she picked up the menu that was placed before her. "Because I love the Caj—" she was cut off Austin.

"Cajun chicken pasta." He took the words right out of her mouth.

"Wow, that is what I was about to say. I can't believe that's your favorite also," she said.

This proved everything Austin knew all along. They were more compatible than any two people could be. "I like the pasta, but actually, *you* are my favorite," Austin flirted.

"Thanks, I'm really flattered." Justice gave him a shy smile.

The waitress approached the table and took their orders. They both ordered the pasta.

"Guess what? Clay and Kiki are getting married," Justice announced.

"Wow, that's good."

"He proposed to her the other day, and, boy, is she excited."

"Congratulate them both for me. I don't know when I'll see them again."

"My auntie is so excited. She is already making a list of people to invite. This wedding will be the social event of Gulfport when she's finished," Justice laughed.

"I'm sure it will be nice."

Justice could tell that Austin had something on his mind. But she wasn't sure if she was ready for it. Had Monica returned and he was calling off the case, or had Morgan changed her mind and decided not to go through with it?

The waitress arrived at the table with their plates and hot garlic cheesy biscuits. Justice's stomach went into overdrive. She was hungry. As soon as the waitress walked away she reached for a biscuit.

"I love these fattening things." Justice took a bite and savored the taste. "So what's up?" she asked.

"I guess you are wondering why I invited you here. And there are two answers. One, I wanted to see you, but these last couple of days have been like murder on me. Two, I want you to know straight-up how I feel about you." He took in a deep breath. "Justice, I'm in love with you."

Justice almost choked on her biscuit.

"Are you OK?" Austin almost jumped out of his seat.

"I'm fine," Justice assured him, then cleared her throat. "Austin, look, you can't be in love with me. You just met me, and please don't feel obligated because of the night we shared."

"Justice, trust me. I know what and how I feel, and I love you. I love everything about you—your smile, the way you walk, talk. To me, you are flawless. And I can't keep pretending that I don't want you in that way, and I'm not referring to passion. I know I am your client and I understand that. But these feelings are real. I want us to be together in a relationship. I'm talking commitment," Austin declared in no uncertain terms.

Justice knew he was telling her nothing but the truth. He was very sincere. And what she hated most was that she felt the same way. But was it possible for them to have a relationship? Unknown to him she was leaving. Gulfport was in her past, and, unfortunately, he would be too.

"Austin, I'm leaving," she blurted at last, feeling relieved as soon as it left her lips. Holding it in was becoming a pressure buildup that she could no longer handle.

"Why? You haven't eaten all of your food," Austin protested, not understanding the context of what she had just released.

"No, Austin. I am leaving Gulfport, soon. I'm moving back to our hometown New York. I have been offered a position as a judge. And I accepted." Justice dropped the ball in plain, simple English so that this time there would be no misunderstanding of what she had said. Austin's shoulders seem to sag. Justice felt awful for telling him this, but she had no choice.

Austin didn't know what to say. This had to be a cruel joke. She had just come into his life. She couldn't be leaving. On one hand, he wanted to congratulate her, but on the other, he wanted to beg her not to go. But that would be selfish, and he could not be selfish. Besides, he loved her and happy is what he ultimately wanted for her. Confusion took over him.

"New York, huh? That's a big accomplishment. Congratulations," Austin managed with a huge knot in his throat. He no longer had the urge to eat. Better yet, swallow anything that could get around the growing knot in his throat.

"Thank you." Justice swallowed the words. She too had lost her appetite, even with all the delicious food placed in front of her she could not eat another bite.

"So we have court Monday. I want you and Morgan to arrive early so that we can consult right before. Other than that, this should be easy."

"Sure." Austin was at a loss for words. "We'll be there on time."

"I really should get back to the office. I have a lot to get done in only a short time. It was nice of you to invite me out." Justice slowly got out of her seat and reached for her purse.

As she turned to leave, Austin found words. "Maybe we can get together again."

"Yeah." Justice looked him square in the eyes and quickly turned to walk away. She had to get out of there. Her heart was sinking, and if she didn't come up for air she would drown. Outside, she took in a big gulp of air and tears clouded her vision as she headed to her car.

Devastated, Austin asked the waitress for the check.

"Would you like a carry box for all the food?" the waitress asked.

Austin didn't answer her because his mind was foggy, but he noticed the waitress standing there. "Did you say something?" he asked her.

"Yes, I asked if you would like carryout boxes," she repeated.

"No, just the check," he managed.

Austin paid the check and left the restaurant. Instead of heading back to the station he went downtown to the park. He needed time to think . . . or at least gather his thoughts.

Chapter Nineteen

As soon as Justice stepped off the elevator she saw Austin and Morgan both sitting in the hallway of the courthouse. She had been running behind all morning. It seemed nothing was going the way she had planned. Candice and Brian had had a fight the night before, and Candice was an emotional wreck over it. Justice did all she could to comfort her before finally telling her she had to get to court. Then she had made it all the way down to her car . . . only to discover she had left the keys on her desk. Talk about pissed, she was it.

"Good morning," Justice greeted both Austin and Morgan as soon as she approached them.

"Good morning," they both replied in unison.

"I'm so sorry I am late. I hope you haven't been waiting long," Justice apologized.

"Actually, we just arrived. I had to run by the station and drop Trent off a file."

"OK. So we're good then," she smiled. "We can go in here and take our seats. The judge should be in the courtroom soon. How do you feel Morgan? Are you ready?"

"Yeah, just a little nervous though." Morgan fidgeted with her hands.

"You'll do fine, sweetheart. The judge will ask you a few questions just to be sure that you aware of the situation today. And then you will be done," Justice explained.

"All right." Morgan gave Justice a smile.

"How about you, Austin, are you OK?" Justice gave him a heartfelt look. Her heart truly ached for him.

"I'm fine," he replied with a smile that was painted on.

"Then you two follow me." Justice led the way to the doors leading into the courtroom. The room was silent. No one was in there beside the bailiff. Justice led Austin and Morgan to the same table she would be sitting at. They sat down slowly while Justice stood. She opened her briefcase and pulled out her files preparing for the judge. Once she had everything out that she needed on the table she sat down right next to Morgan. Austin had sat at the end of the table. He seemed to be in his own world. Although Justice knew he couldn't wait to get full custody of Morgan, she knew he was disturbed about her move to New York.

The bailiff finally told them to stand for the judge as the judge walked in. After the bailiff's normal speech about which judge was presiding, blah, blah, blah, they were all reseated.

"Council, you may approach," the judge said.

Justice made her way to the podium to speak with the judge.

"Council, this is a custody case if I understand correctly."

"Yes, Judge Robinson."

"Are there any other parties involved? Because if not, I would like to make this brief. I start my vacation right after." Judge Robinson didn't smile, but Justice knew he was serious and wanted to smile. He was a family man and one of the nicest judges she knew. If there was ever a joke to be made, he was the one to make it.

"I understand your situation, Your Honor, so let's make this quick." Justice winked her eye at him. She remembered her very first case was held in Judge Robinson's courtroom. He had made several sarcastic remarks, and Justice was on the verge of a breakdown when Judge Robinson called her to his podium and told her, "Welcome aboard, Council. Lighten up. I'm only your first judge." Justice walked away from the podium feeling relaxed and nailed her first case. And she always thanked Judge Robinson for that. His sarcasm had made her argument more drastic.

"You may step back, Council, and proceed."

"Your Honor, we are here today to render full custody of Morgan Crews to present parent Austin Crews. Mr. Crews, as of now, has been issued temporary custody. Absent parent Monica Jones is still absent and has been for over a month with no contact. And as in the petition previously filed, Ms. Jones has a history of leaving for months at a time, then returning to claim Morgan Crews. This is causing emotional distress to the young client Morgan Crews, who deserves, Your Honor, to have a stable environment." Justice paused. "I have nothing further, Your Honor."

"OK, Council, has the absent parent been notified of this hearing today?"

"Ms. Jones has been unreachable to this point. We have tried all communication possible to reach her, but to no avail. We have exhausted all attempts."

"Then let's see." Judge Robinson seemed to pause while studying the file in front of him. "Morgan Crews, can I have you come up and take a seat on the stand."

Morgan looked at Austin who gave her a reassuring nod. She pushed her chair back and slowly walked up to the stand. Then she looked out at Justice and Austin and afterward, turned to look directly at Judge Robinson.

"Young lady, I am Judge Robinson, and I would like to ask you a couple of questions. And you don't have to be scared or nervous because I don't bite." Judge Robinson made an attempt to calm Morgan's nerves. "How long have you been staying with your father?"

"For the last two months," Morgan answered, and to Justice's surprise, she didn't sound the least bit nervous.

"How would you like living with him permanently, for good, or at least until you're eighteen?" Judge Robinson asked.

"I would love to. He takes good care of me." Morgan looked out at Austin and smiled.

"What about your mom?" Judge Robinson changed the conversation. "What if she returned tonight and she wanted you to return home with her? How would you feel about that?"

Morgan looked down at her hands for a while. A tear ran down her right cheek. Justice could tell Austin wanted to get up and protect her. Justice looked over at Austin and only moving her lips she told him, "She will be OK." Morgan looked at Judge Robinson.

"Judge, I love my mom. There's not a night that I go to sleep that I don't miss her. Sometimes I miss her so much I cry. But Dad is always there for me, loving me, and making sure I'm OK. We take care of each other, and that's what I want. At this time, my mother, for whatever reason, can't give me that. And I understand. So if she was to return tonight, she would have to take me kicking and screaming because I won't leave my dad." Morgan at that point had a face that was dripping with tears.

Judge Robinson just stared at her as if he couldn't believe she was the same girl who had slowly and nervously walked to the stand only moments before. "Young lady, that was very well put." He smiled at Morgan.

"Council, I think that brings this to an end. Mr. Crews, I am hereby granting you full custody of your daughter, Morgan Crews. Morgan, you may step down and go home with your dad, forever."

"Thank you," Morgan said with a sniffle.

Austin stood up and met Morgan in the middle of the room and gave her a big hug.

"We did it, Dad. We won."

"Yes, baby, we did."

The happiness on their faces sent tears racing down Justice's face.

"Thank you so much, Justice." Morgan walked over and gave her a hug.

"You don't have to thank me, sweetheart. I would do it all over again just to see you smile."

"No, we do have to thank you. So thank you," Austin said.

"You're welcome."

"How about you let us take you out to dinner to celebrate?" Austin asked.

"Yeah, we could do Sal's Pizzeria," Morgan beamed.

Justice hesitated. She had so much to do in such little time there was no way she could make it.

"Actually, I can't. Sounds good, but I . . . I have so much to do. I'm leaving in a couple of days for New York. And I have all this packing to get done before I leave. I don't have a minute to spare."

"New York? That sounds fun," Morgan smiled. "When are you coming back?"

Justice looked at Austin. For some reason she figured he would tell Morgan about the move.

"Sweetheart, I'm moving there for good. I'm going to be a judge over there. Can you imagine that?" Justice gave a slight smile. She could tell that Morgan was sad.

"But we just met. I thought you could take me out some more. Just us, you and me," Morgan gestured to Justice, then back at herself.

"Morgan, where are your manners? You should be congratulating Justice on her job, not making her feel guilty about leaving."

"I'm sorry, Justice. I didn't mean to," Morgan apologized.

"It' OK. And don't worry, I'll see you again."

"OK," Morgan replied. She was crushed. Just as she had opened up to Justice, now she was leaving. She would miss having Justice around. She felt that with her mother being gone she now had someone to talk to about girl problems. But more than anything, she felt sorry for her dad because she knew how he felt about Justice. Although he tried his best to keep it from her she knew.

The room seemed to fill up with deafening silence. Austin was suffocating. He had to get out.

"Well, we won't hold you up," he spoke up first.

Justice had decided the best way to handle the situation was to remain professional, even if she was screaming and crying inside. "Tabitha will have some papers for you later today, and you can swing by and pick them up. And I'll be seeing both of you before I leave." Justice grabbed her briefcase off the table and left the room. Her dream was calling her, and if she wanted to get closer to it, she had to pack herself up. No time for wasted tears. She had done exactly what she set out to do with Austin Crews. She had obtained full custody for him of Morgan. At least she could go to New York knowing they were together and that no one could separate them again.

Chapter Twenty

After leaving court, Austin had taken Morgan out to Sal's Pizzeria to grab a pizza. They sat down and talked about their victory on the custody battle. Neither one brought up Justice and the fact that she was leaving. Austin tried very hard to push it out of his mind so that he could concentrate on being happy. He finally had full legal custody of Morgan at this very moment. Nothing for him could be better. So after laughing and talking, they went home.

Austin plopped down on the couch in the den to watch some television. After flipping through every channel on the TV, he decided there wasn't a decent movie in sight. So he settled on ESPN, but after listening to the sportscaster rant and rave about this and that, Austin realized the guy was annoying him because his mind was solely on Justice. He was trying so hard to push her to the back and let it go. She was moving to New York, and there was nothing he could do to change that. The one woman that he managed to fall head over heels in love with was leaving town moving to a whole other state. After Monica, he thought he could never love anyone else that way, but he was wrong. He loved Justice more. She was everything he thought a woman should be, and now she was walking right out of his life. Austin had been so wrapped up in his thoughts that he hadn't noticed Morgan enter the living room.

"Dad," Morgan called his name.

"Yes, Pumpkin?" Austin looked up at her. He felt like his mind was racing and he couldn't control it. But he managed to give Morgan his undivided attention.

"Can you take me over to visit Tammy? She has a couple of new movies and Ms. Sylvia said it was OK for me to come over. So can I go?" Morgan pleaded with her eyes.

Austin could never resist Morgan when she gave him those eyes. "Sure, Pumpkin, let me grab my keys." Austin bounced off the couch.

Morgan knew her dad was sad about Justice leaving. He had not admitted to her yet, but she knew that he was in love with Justice. She knew that he didn't tell her because he thought that she would be upset. But she loved Justice, and she would love for them to be together. She had secretly wished they were married so that way she and Tammy be could be cousins. Morgan didn't have any family in Gulfp Port, Mississippi, any more. The few that used to live there had moved away to other parts of the state. So she only had friends, but she and Tammy were closer than any of her other friends had ever been. They were two peas in a pod.

"Dad, I know I am only twelve, but if you love someone you just don't let them walk out of your life."

Austin had just stopped at a red light. He looked over at Morgan. "I know," he replied, not sure where Morgan was going with this.

"Then do something, Dad."

Austin was even more confused. "Pumpkin, you have my undivided attention, but what are you talking about?" Austin gave her a smile.

"Justice," Morgan said. "Dad, if you love her, then don't let her leave you."

Austin was shocked. He had no idea that Morgan knew how he felt about Justice. "How did you know?" he asked.

"Because." Morgan paused. "I have seen how you are around her, and besides, she loves you back."

"Well, I guess none of that matters because she's leaving. And I can't change that." Austin pulled in Sylvia's driveway. Tammy was already standing outside waiting when they arrived.

Morgan gave her dad a stern look. "Yes, you can. Isn't it you who is always telling me anything is possible. So now I am telling you." Morgan beamed giving her dad her most precious smile.

"Thanks, Pumpkin, but I will be fine. I want you to go enjoy yourself and not worry about me. Call me when you're ready."

"I will. And, Dad, go get her." Morgan reached over and gave him a peck on the cheek and jumped out of the car.

Tammy and Morgan waved him off as he backed out of the driveway and headed for home and ESPN.

ððð

Austin wasn't sure when he had made up his mind to go to Justice's house. But before he knew it, he was sitting outside parked in her driveway. From the looks of it, she wasn't home. Not one of her vehicles was in sight. But they could have been parked in the garage. Either way, if she wasn't home he would find her. His mind was made up.

Justice was surprised when her doorbell rang. She hadn't been expecting anyone. She was in high swing of packing her things and trying to shake Austin out of her mind. And possibly her heart one day. Maybe.

"Hey," Justice spoke when she opened the door. She was sure he could see the embarrassed look on her face. "What are you doing here?" Justice almost hated the words as they left her mouth. She didn't mean it the way it came out, but she looked a mess. Her hair was in a straggly ponytail, and she had on a sweat suit because the last person she was expecting to show up at her door was Austin.

"I'm sorry to show up unannounced, but I had to see you." The look in his eyes tugged at her heart. She wanted to comfort him, let him know that everything would be all right. But she felt that was a lie.

"Come on in." Justice stepped aside. "I just wasn't expecting any company," she said. She tried to pull all the loose strings back into her ponytail.

Austin turned around to face her. "Can we sit somewhere and talk?"

"Sure." Justice led the way to her den area where she had on one of her Jagged Edge CDs. Things were everywhere. She had been trying to pack up a few things before the movers came. "I'm sorry it looks a mess in here but packing can be treacherous." Justice went to move a box out in front of the couch so they could sit down.

"No, let me get that." Austin reached down and started to move the box.

"So where is Morgan?" Justice asked.

"I just dropped her at Tammy's house." Austin smiled as he maneuvered the box to the other side of the room.

"That figures," Justice replied. "Can I get you something to drink?"

"Just your undivided attention if I may." Austin looked her dead in the eyes.

A little hesitant at first Justice agreed. "OK."

Austin walked over and took her hand and led her over to have a seat on the couch.

"I know you have this big commitment to following your dreams a hundred percent, and I support you and I understand. I would never ask you to give up your dream for me. But what I will ask you to do is to love me. Because I love you with every part of my being. Justice, I have loved you ever since the first day I bumped into you at the courthouse. Do you remember that?"

To control her tears Justice decided not to speak so she just nodded her head yes.

"And that's why I want you to marry me," Austin said, as tears spilled down both his cheeks.

Shocked, Justice covered her mouth in awe as tears started rolling down her face like a waterfall, none of which she could control.

"Please marry me." Austin begged. "I will move to New York. Morgan and I both. We will pack up and just move there."

Justice started to shake her head. "No, I can't let you do that."

"It won't be a problem. There's a precinct in New York that's starting up a new division. They have been begging me to come out and head up that division. But with all the madness with Monica I hadn't made up my mind. But now that is over and I have custody of Morgan, so this could be great."

"That's just it. You can't up and move Morgan away. Away from all her friends. She will be devastated. For once she has a chance to have a stable home; no moving around. I can't do that to her. No, I *won't* do that her." Justice's mind was made up. "Austin, I love you, and nothing would make me happier than to marry you." She stood up and wiped her face, but the tears kept coming.

"So you *do* love me? That's the first time I ever heard you say it."

"Yes, I do, but we can't be together." Her words were like a punch to the gut for Austin. "We both know a long-distance relationship won't work." Justice felt she was being realistic.

Austin silently looked off in the distance for at least three minutes. "So I guess that's it."

Justice nodded her head yes, not wanting to say anything else.

"When can I see you before you leave? I would like to say good-bye."

"Oh about that, I was going to call you tonight to let you know that my flight leaves the day after tomorrow. They need me to arrive a few days earlier than planned. Can you hug Morgan for me? Tell her once I get settled I'll write to her."

With a distant look in his eyes, Austin found his voice. "I'll do that." He looked at Justice long and hard, then headed toward the door.

Weak in the knees, Justice headed straight to her kitchen and grabbed a bottle of wine and a tall glass. There was no way she would get anything else packed. She needed to clear her mind and a bottle of wine would do just that. She turned up Jagged Edge and popped the cork.

Chapter Twenty-One

Ding dong, ding dong.

Justice was awakened by the doorbell. She looked about the room at all the stuff still waiting to be packed. The empty bottle of wine was still on the table. That's when she realized she must have dozed off the whole night after drinking the entire bottle of wine. After Austin left she had drunk glass after glass of wine until she thought she felt better. But the piercing pain that shot through her head made it clear she had a slight hangover and the empty feeling in her heart let her know nothing was resolved.

Before she could get off the couch the bell rang again. "Shit," Justice said aloud wishing whoever it was would stop ringing the darn bell. She made her way to the front door, then realized it must have been Aunt Mattie and Kiki coming over to help her pack some things.

"What took you so long?" Kiki asked as soon as the door swung open. "Wait a minute, are still in here asleep?" Kiki observed the slumber look on Justice's face.

"I guess you could say that." Justice ran her hand through her hair that hung in her face, completely disheveled. "Good morning, Auntie."

"Good morning, baby." Aunt Mattie reached for a hug as always. She was a very lovable person. Justice would miss her terribly when she moved to New York.

"I'm glad you guys showed up. I actually don't have that much more to do. The movers are going to pack up most of this stuff. The rest won't come until spring. By then, the house should be sold."

Walking in ahead of them Kiki reached the kitchen first. "What do you mean you don't have a lot? *Look* at this kitchen. And I know you are not going to trust no movers to pack up your crystal." Kiki pointed to some of Justice's expensive beveled crystal glasses.

"Kiki, they are professionals. They won't break anything; besides, it's all insured."

"Umm, aren't we the nonchalant one this morning?" Kiki said sarcastically.

"Justice, don't pay your cousin no nevermind. What do you need us to do?" Auntie Mattie said, giving Kiki a threatening look.

"We can start upstairs with my clothes and shoes. Those things I would like to pack myself."

"I tell you what, let me whip you up something real quick to eat first. Then we can get started," Aunt Mattie said.

"All right. I'm going to jump in the shower and get cleaned up and I'll be right back down."

Slowly Justice climbed her stairs and took a long, hot shower. Allowing the water to trickle down her body she tried to think happy thoughts about New York and her new position as a judge. She was happy but not as happy as she knew she should be. After showering, she threw on some

Seven Jeans and a wife beater shirt and ran back downstairs. She didn't realize how hungry she was until she smelled the bacon her auntie was frying.

"Umm, Auntie, that smells so good. I'm going to miss your cooking," Justice whined.

"Don't worry, Justice, I'm sure New York has a lot of greasy spoons where you can pick up some good soul food," Kiki responded while pouring herself some Tropicana orange juice she had fished out of the fridge.

"That's not real cooking. It will only clog her arteries. Now you look here, baby, you stay away from those greasy spoons, ya hear?" Aunt Mattie warned her.

"I'll do my best, Auntie." Justice gave her a smile.

"Auntie, what do you expect her to eat? You know that Justice don't cook."

"Yes, I do, you cow," Justice laughed.

"You two come on over here and grab some of this food." Aunt Mattie set two plates of bacon, eggs, toast, and grits on the table.

They sat, ate, and talked about New York and about all the monuments and the Statue of Liberty. Auntie Mattie said she couldn't wait to come for a visit. Then it was upstairs to Justice's room to pack.

"So have you decided where the wedding is going to be held?" Justice asked Kiki. "And please don't tell me at that god-awful park."

"Oh, God, Justice, what made you think of that?" Kiki laughed.

"You think I forgot? I can remember when we were teenagers, that was all you used to talk about. About how your wedding was going to be held at Ricker's Park. Even then I thought that was a horrible, horrible, idea. And as an adult I really can't imagine it." Justice laughed so hard her full stomach hurt.

Kiki smiled thinking back to all her childish plans for a wedding. "No, after years of growing up, I have decided to let the park thing go." Kiki grinned, still thinking about her old wishes.

"Thank God." Justice held up holy hands to the ceiling as if she was in worship service.

"Now I am thinking more of Hedler's Hall. That place is absolutely beautiful."

Justice remembered the first time she had became a member of that country club. The place was absolutely breathtaking, the perfect place to say "I do."

"It is. Oh, Kiki, I'm so happy for you. My little cousin is getting married." Justice walked over and hugged Kiki tight. When Justice went to let go of the embrace Kiki held on for a little longer. When she finally let go Justice could tell she was crying.

"I'm going to miss you sooo much." Kiki wiped at the tears running down her face.

"I'm going to miss you too." Justice started to cry. They both stood there wiping tears off their face. While they had been bawling, Aunt Mattie had gone to the bathroom to retrieve Kleenex for both of them.

"Thanks, Auntie," Justice said as she reached for her Kleenex. "Look at us, we act like we won't ever see each other again."

"I know, right?" Kiki continued to dab at her never-ending tears.

After the tears dried, they started back to packing. Aunt Mattie was folding the clothes as they brought them out of the closet. Justice had brought in a few boxes that she picked up from Lowe's.

"Justice, how did court go for that sweet Morgan? She's such a lovely child," Aunt Mattie complimented.

"Austin has full custody, now." Justice kept packing, deciding not to go into too much detail. The last person she wanted to discuss was Austin. She needed to focus on something else—anything else.

"Ain't that a blessing? Well, you tell the both of them I said congratulations. Sylvia says that she is such a respectful child." Aunt Mattie shook her head. "And too bad I won't get to know Austin. I really like him."

"Yeah, too bad he won't be in the family," Kiki said as she headed into the back of the huge closet.

Justice decided to ignore Kiki because she knew she was only being sarcastic to get a response. And Justice knew that at that point if she did respond she would fall apart. She was trying very hard to not dwell on Austin; it was tough enough.

"So are you going to tell us what he was doing over yesterday? Or do I have to drag it out of you?" Kiki babbled, demanding an answer.

"How do you know Austin was here yesterday? What were you doing, stalking me?" Justice asked.

"I wouldn't exactly call it stalking, but yesterday I decided to come by and help out since I got off work early. I thought that maybe I would help you pack a lot more if I came a day early. But when I got here I saw Austin's truck parked outside in your driveway. So instead of knocking on your door and interrupting you guys, I decided to wait until today. I thought maybe you were going over the case with him and Morgan. However, as I was pulling off from your house, Aunt Sylvia called and asked me to drop her off some paprika. That's when I discovered sweet little Morgan who happened to be over to visit with Tammy." Kiki raised her left eyebrow. Justice hated when she did that she because she was so good at it. And no matter how much Justice practiced it, the only thing that ever would raise was her whole face.

"Look, you don't have to do the eyebrow thing with me. I'll tell you." Justice decided to lay it out on the line since Kiki let her know on all levels she was busted.

"Austin and I are in love," Justice blurted. At that point she didn't realize that she was going to say that. But it actually felt right when she said it.

Aunt Mattie dropped the shirt she had been folding. "Repeat that, baby," Aunt Mattie said to be sure she understood Justice.

"We are in love," Justice said clearly.

"I knew it, I knew it! And all that time you spent trying to deny it. What a waste," Kiki laughed. "What does he think about your moving all the way to New York?"

"That's why he was here yesterday. He came over to propose. He asked me if I would marry him."

Aunt Mattie gasped and grabbed her chest. Kiki and Justice both ran to her. "What's wrong, Auntie?" Justice asked first.

Aunt Mattie cleared her throat. "Ain't nothing wrong, but I thought you said he asked you marry him."

"He did, Auntie," Justice clarified.

"Oh my Lord, two weddings. Thank you, Jesus. This is what I been on my knees asking you for. I always knew you would answer my prayer," Aunt Mattie said looking toward the heavens.

"Auntie, there is not going to be two weddings because I turned him down."

"Why?" Kiki asked in shock.

"You know why. Because I'm moving to New York tomorrow, Kiki. And I don't know if that is logical to you, but that might have something to do with it," Justice answered sarcastically.

"Sorry. You don't have to bite my head off," Kiki apologized, and Justice instantly felt bad.

"Wait, I'm sorry, Kiki, I didn't mean that."

"It's OK. I shouldn't ask you crazy questions. I just think it's so romantic of him to propose to keep you here in Gulfport."

"That's just it. He actually offered to move to New York. There is a job all ready there waiting for him if he wants it."

"Really?" Kiki smiled. "So then, what's the problem?" she wanted to know.

Tears again started to dispense down Justice's face. "Can't you see, Kiki, I can't do that to him or to Morgan. Especially not to Morgan. I can't allow them to pack up their lives and move all the way to New York just to accommodate me. Morgan has all her friends here and for the first time she has a family home that is stable. It would be selfish of me to let them do this."

Kiki looked to her auntie for help. because she just didn't understand her cousin. How could she let something so good pass her by? The man had offered to move to New York with her so that they could be man and wife. How she could turn that down?

"Come here, Justice." Aunt Mattie called her over to where she was sitting on the bed. She reached for both of Justice's hands and placed them in hers. "Honey, when are you going to allow yourself happiness again, huh? You walk around with Keith on your back allowing what he did to you to heave on your soul. You can't live your life like that. At some point you have to allow Justice some happiness. And I'm not just talking about your career, I'm talking about personnel things that fulfill you outside of a career. You are already successful there. Life is short, honey; live it and enjoy yourself. Take some chances, maybe even drastic ones. Step out of your shell for once.

"Now you just told me you love this man who is willing to relocate his job while uprooting his daughter just to be wit' cha. That's love, baby. Stop trying to find excuses to block it." Aunt Mattie gave her an assuring smile.

"Justice, go after him and accept his proposal. Trust me, it's the right decision," Kiki added to Aunt Mattie's advice.

Justice slowly released her hands from her aunt's and walked back toward the closet, but she turned around to look at Kiki. "No, Kiki, the right decision is for me to look to my future. I have to focus on me. I can't jeopardize that. Keith taught me that."

"He's not Keith, Justice. Get that through your thick head." Kiki rested her case.

"I already have, so don't forget to meet me at the airport tomorrow. They will be shipping my Range Rover off tomorrow right before my flight at noon." Justice changed the subject and disappeared into her walk-in closet.

That was the end of the conversation. The rest of the packing was done in silence. And after packing up all the clothes they gave in and just decided to let the packers finish all the rest. Besides, everything wouldn't be shipped now because Justice would be in a hotel when she first arrived in New York. Aunt Mattie and Kiki decided it was getting late and they should get going. After they left, Justice was so tired she lay down on her bed to gather her thoughts before dozing off. Morning was upon her before she knew it. After taking a quick shower and taking her luggage down the stairs she decided to grab a bagel before rushing out the door to meet Kiki and Aunt Mattie at the airport to say their good-byes.

Chapter Twenty-Two

A full month in New York and Justice was still trying to find her comfort zone. Each day was the same as the day before: a car would pick her up and take her downtown to the Civil Courthouse in Manhattan. That is where she worked and where she would be sworn in as judge in a short two weeks. The district judge Phillip Wagner and the board had spared no expense bringing Justice to New York. She had an unlimited company credit card for food and expenses, access to the company jet, a full membership to the country club, and was being paid an eight-figure salary. They made it no secret that she was wanted by rolling out the red carpet. Her office overlooked Manhattan with a VIP view located on the fourteenth floor. Justice had forgotten how tall and extravagant buildings in New York could be.

Her next goal was to get out of the hotel she had been staying in since she had arrived there. They had put her up in the Ritz Carlton with a year setup stay if she so wished. But Justice couldn't imagine living in a hotel for a year. While she enjoyed the room service, she needed a home, someplace that she could feel settled. Staying at the hotel made her feel like a visitor, like she would be leaving soon. So with that in mind she got a realtor to help her find a place that would be accessible to the courthouse right in Manhattan. She would rent for now, and later, she would buy a home. And under her realtor guidance expert, Scott Hamilton, she had found and fell in love with the Riverhouse Penthouse. It was in the center of Manhattan so she wouldn't have to take any taxis to get to the courthouse. She would also have access to a car garage to park her Range Rover which had been in storage since she had arrived in New York. She had left the Silver Mercedes along with her candy apple red Benz that Keith had purchased for her in the car garage back in Gulfport.

Since the move she was seriously thinking about selling the Benz. It only took her back down memory lane with Keith. And that lane was over and done with. No more sadness or migraine headaches. The Keith Syndrome had run its course. So on her trip back to Gulfport, selling the Benz was definitely on the top of her to-do list, along with selling her house which was already on the market. Scott, her realtor, had already given her some advice on selling a car such as a Benz.

Scott had become a friend since her arrival in New York, so after finding her penthouse, they decided to go out and celebrate. Justice didn't know much about the city's hot restaurants so Scott had offered to pick her up. So after throwingShe threw on a one-strap black Prada dress that stopped at the knees and pumps to match. Justice considered herself ready. Just as she retrieved a bag to match her outfit, she heard the doorman buzz. The building was very exclusive. Security was tight. No one could just walk in to visit. That was one of the reasons Justice had chosen it. Being single and alone in the big city she wanted to feel safe.

"Ms. Lopez, you have a Mr. Scott Hamilton here," Papeto, the doorman, alerted her.

"Sure, send him up," Justice replied.

Within minutes Scott was at the door. Justice opened the door with a smile ready to go. But when she opened the door she noticed Scott had a shocked look on his face. However, she chalked it up to her appearance. Normally when he saw her she was dressed in jeans to go house hunting.

"Wow, you look stunning," he complimented.

"You think so? I thought I would throw on something besides jeans tonight."

"Good choice," he smiled.

"Well, let's get going." Justice closed the door behind her.

Once outside Justice noticed Scott had chosen to have a limo escort them. She wasn't shocked though. While Scott was a licensed realtor he actually owned the company. That's why she was surprised when she found out the owner was taking her house hunting. The day she had gone in to get started she had met with a woman, but a day later, she found out that Scott himself would be taking her around.

"So I thought we would do a little dancing, and then dinner at one of the finest restaurants in New York," Scott informed her. "If that is OK with you."

"I just want to have a good time," Justice replied with a smile. Tonight would be good for her. She would enjoy herself. She had a new place that she could call home. And she wouldn't be sitting at home thinking about Gulfport, her family, and Austin. As much as she had tried to shake Austin since New York, she couldn't. She couldn't even find the courage to write Morgan like she had promised. So tonight she would have fun with a new friend and not think about any of that.

After arriving at a club that was famous for Salsa dancing Justice kicked back, had some drinks, danced, and relaxed. Dinner was just as exciting. They dined on some fine cuisine, much of it Justice had not tried in a long time. Scott made her feel comfortable. He told her a little about his life and how he had come to own his own realtor company. Justice gave him a little of her background in Gulfport, leaving out Austin. She didn't feel the need to discuss that with anyone. Besides, she nearly broke down each time she thought about him. So the conversation was nice, the food was good, but soon it was time to go home.

When they arrived back at the hotel, Scott walked Justice back up to her door. After saying good night, much to her shock, he reached out to kiss Justice, but she moved just in time to avoid the contact.

Scott immediately felt embarrassed. "Wait . . . I'm sorry. I shouldn't have done that without asking you," he apologized.

"It's OK. I'm just not ready for that," Justice informed him adequately.

"I think I should be honest with you," Scott said.

Justice was confused. She didn't know what he would have to be honest with her about. They had only known each other for a couple of weeks. And in that time it had been strictly business, or so she thought.

"The . . ." Scott paused, "the first time I saw you wasn't the day we met at the condo I showed you."

Justice gave him a look of confusion because she wasn't sure where he was going with this confession.

"The first time you came into the office to start the process was when I saw you. I got a glimpse of you going into Maxine's office, the realtor you met with. After you left I told her that I would take you house hunting and that if there was a sell, she would get the proceeds." Scott paused again, fidgeting with his hands. "You see, Justice, I don't normally show houses or condos. Penthouses." He pointed toward her door with a grin. "But from the moment I saw you I knew I had to meet you." Scott looked Justice square in the face, and Justice knew he was sincere. That would explain what happened to the realtor she had originally met with. She thought it strange that the owner would be showing her places, but she had dismissed the thought so quickly she never gave it a second speculation. Maybe she hadn't speculated much because Scott was white. And living in Gulfport she had gotten used to the fact that there was no interracial dating. In other words, she didn't have to wonder about a white man wanting to date her. But this was New York. Interracial dating was part of their culture. Almost. However, she just wasn't interested in Scott, or any other man, for the matter. She had to get Austin out of her heart first.

"Wow, Scott, that's a lot. But . . . I should be honest with you. I am not looking for a relationship . . . period.

Moving here I left someone behind and I . . ." Justice paused again, her emotional feelings were taking over. "I'm just not ready to open up that chapter in my life. Right now I need to focus on my career. I'm sorry." Justice turned to unlock her door.

Scott gently reached for her arm. And Justice turned back to face him. "You take all the time you need, but if you change your mind, you know where to find me."

With that Justice opened her door and stepped into her beautifully furnished penthouse. Her emotions were running high. Scott's confession only made Justice miss Austin that much more. She loved him, and she still had no idea how she would adjust without him.

ðð ð

The day had come for Justice to be sworn in, and she couldn't believe it. She got up and got dressed with a surreal feeling. Even though she had been going to the courthouse every day, sitting in her office at her desk, it just wasn't the same. After making it to the courthouse her assistant Maya had brought her in a plate of mixed fruit and yogurt.

Finally the moment came for the swearing in, and it was everything she dreamed it would be . . . and more. For the first time she felt fulfillment in New York. Afterward, they took a lot of pictures with different judges on her panel. She was welcomed and hugged by so many people she thought her family was there. Now she had a family, her cojudges They had a commitment to each other, and she would not disappoint. And they had another surprise for her. The whole time she had been there they had been calling her by Lopez, her last name which she hated.

After the picture taking the celebration kicked off, and the district judge gave a toast and told her that she would be addressed by her first name, Justice, as she so wished. She was so shocked that she cried. Mr. Rhem and Garrett had told them this was her desire because she had not yet found the courage to do so. But she cringed inwardly every time someone addressed her as Lopez. Finally the swearing in and celebrations were over. Justice had received four robes. She decided to leave three at the office and take one home to hang in her closet to look at whenever she pleased. She threw her robe across her arm and headed out into the night.

Back at the penthouse her fatigue started in. On the elevator ride up she yawned. Her eyes were really starting to feel heavy. But it seemed the elevator kept stopping to let someone on or let someone off. She secretly wished the door wouldn't stop again. Finally on the sixth floor the last person got off. The last stop would be the twelfth floor, to her penthouse, but soon the red button flashed and on the tenth floor the door popped open. And none other than P. Diddy stepped on the elevator. Shocked, Justice didn't speak. She didn't want him to think she was some type of crazed fan because actually she wasn't.

"Hi." He spoke first, pressing the first-floor button without looking at the number.

"Hi," Justice replied, turning her attention back to the elevator buttons wanting to scream at him for taking them back down.

In silence the elevator headed back down, stalling on the fourth floor this time.

"I'm P. Diddy, and you are . . .?" he asked.

"Justice," she replied without emotion.

"Wait, is that your name?" he smiled.

"Yeah." Justice wasn't shocked. She got that a lot when people found out her name.

"Wow, never met anyone with that name before." Just then the elevator stopped on the first floor and the doors opened.

That's when he noticed he pushed the wrong floor. "Ah, my bad. I hit the wrong button. I'm going up." Justice gave him a look of frustration as he pressed his button.

"So are you in a choir or something?" He pointed toward her robe.

"No." Justice's answer was short. She wanted off the elevator regardless of who was on it.

"What's with the robe then?" He was curious.

"I was sworn in today. I'm a judge." Justice felt proud.

"Wow, congratulations. Imagine that, a judge with the name Justice. What a coincidence."

"Thank you." Justice smiled for the first time.

"Well, I have a penthouse in this building on the twelfth floor." He gave her the room number as the elevator stopped.

"Actually, I live on this same floor," she informed him without intention.

"OK, cool. You are welcome to stop by anytime. I never know which crib I'm going to use when I'm in town. But here is my number if you want to call first." He handed her a card with his cell and business numbers on it. "It was really nice meeting you, Justice. I hope I see you again."

"Nice meeting you too," she replied.

With that, they both headed in opposite directions toward their respective penthouse. Justice didn't know what to think about what had just happened. Even more, she didn't know why he had given her his numbers. She had no reason to want to call him. She didn't even listen to his music. Once inside her apartment she shrugged it off because stranger things had happened. She headed upstairs to her room where she threw herself across her bed.

The ringing of her cell phone woke her up. The ring tone was that of Kiki. She looked at the clock which told her it was six o'clock in the morning. She immediately sat up in the bed with a racing heart. Something must have been wrong.

"What's up, Kiki?" Justice said in the phone right away with her left hand on her pounding her heart which she was sure would bust at any moment.

"Why didn't you call me last night when you got in from your swearing-in?" Kiki yelled on the other end of the phone.

"Kiki, is everything all right, girl?" Justice asked trying to calm her fast beating heart down.

"Yeah, everything is fine," she said still wanting an answer.

"Girl, don't scare me like that. Calling me this early in the morning I thought something was wrong with Auntie," Justice released with a sigh.

"Calm down, Justice. Auntie is fine. But what I want to know is why you didn't call me."

"I'm sorry, but when I talked to Auntie on the way from the courthouse last night she told me you were out with Clay. So I decided to wait; besides, when I got in, I fell asleep. I was tired from the celebration they gave me."

"So how does it feel to be a *judge?*" Kiki emphasized the word.

"Oh, Kiki, it feels wonderful. I'm on top of the world," Justice smiled. "But I just hate you guys couldn't be here." Justice missed them terribly.

"We wanted to, but you know Dr. Shapiro don't want Auntie traveling right now. He stressed that in his orders."

Justice sighed knowing it could not be helped."I know. So how is the wedding planning going?" she decided to change the subject.

"Great. But I am overwhelmed. I wish you were here to help me. Aunt Sylvia and Renee have helped me a lot."

"Good. What does Clay think?" Justice ask.

"He doesn't care. Everything is my decision. Whatever I want he just says fine." Kiki beamed. "So how are things there? Are you getting out seeing the big city? Please don't tell me it's all work and home." Kiki was sarcastic on purpose.

"I get out. I go to lunch, and I went shopping for furniture for my new penthouse," Justice revealed.

"You have a penthouse? Ahhhh!" Kiki yelled with excitement through the phone. "Now I can't wait to come for a visit. Is it in Manhattan?"

"Heck, yeah."

"Justice, you are going to meet all the celebrities." Kiki was really excited.

Just then Justice thought about P. Diddy. It had completely slipped her mind. "I already have. I met P. Diddy last night."

"Get. Out!" Kiki yelled again. "You are lying, Justice."

"I swear. He has a penthouse on the same floor as me. I met him last night in the elevator. He gave me his number and everything."

All Justice could hear was Kiki screaming in the background. She must have dropped the phone. Finally she picked it back up.

"Justice, you have to take me to him when I visit," Kiki demanded.

"I will, but please don't act this excited in front of your fiancé. He might get the impression that you love P. Diddy more than you love him," Justice teased.

"My bad. I guess I did get carried away. But there is no way I could love anyone the way I love my Clay. He is my dream come true. I kick myself everytime I think about the losers I had to date just to find my prince charming." Justice could hear the smile in her voice. "So you are still coming to the wedding, because if you don't, I will kill you," Kiki threatened.

"I wouldn't miss it for the world. I already have my flight booked."

"Good." She got quiet. "So have you talked to Austin?" Kiki pried, even though she knew the answer.

Justice knew she would bring up Austin. She had tried to think of what she would say but that all depended on the question. And now here it was, right out front.

"No, I have not," Justice admitted.

"Why, Justice?" Kiki asked. "You know he misses you."

Justice got quiet. She didn't know what to say.

"Well, he hasn't called me either. My number is the same. It has not changed. Besides, maybe he has moved on with his life." Justice got defensive.

"Nonsense, Justice, you know better." Kiki defended Austin. "I saw Morgan over at Aunt Sylvia's house, and she asked about you. She said you were going to write to her. Have you written her yet?"

"I haven't had the time," Justice lied.

"Well, you should. She really cares about you," Kiki informed her.

Justice felt bad enough. She didn't know why Kiki had to hit her with that. Kiki knew how Justice felt about Morgan.

"Well, I have to get going. I have to be at the office in a couple of hours." Justice wanted to end the call on that note.

"OK, I'll let you go." Kiki felt bad putting the guilt on Justice. "And, Justice, I'm sorry. I didn't to mean make you feel bad about Morgan."

"It's OK. I know you mean well. Kiss Auntie for me, OK?" Justice requested.

"All right," Kiki said.

After hanging up Justice got up and took a long hot shower before heading out. She had a lot to think about. Her trip would be coming up soon, and she would need to do some shopping for gifts for her family. Kiki had fitted her for her dress before she came out to New York so that was taken care of. She would be the maid of honor. Justice couldn't wait to stand by her cousin's side on her most special day.

Chapter Twenty-Three

As soon as Justice's flight touched down in Gulfport she felt relieved. She had been waiting for this moment even before she boarded the plane headed to New York. Kiki's wedding. It was raining and gloomy looking outside. Justice hoped it wouldn't look like this on Kiki's wedding day. Thank God the wedding was being held inside a building. Justice had talked to Kiki the day before, and according to her, it had been raining all week long.

"Justice!," Kiki yelled as soon as Justice came through gate eight.

Justice ran to Kiki and they hugged so tight.

"I missed you so much," Justice cried.

"I missed you too." They continued to hug each other. They had not been apart that long since Justice had gone off to college.

"Let's get you over to Aunt Mattie's. She can't wait to see you. She wanted to come to the airport, but I talked her out of it. I didn't think she needed to be out in this cold wet air," Kiki explained.

They jumped in Kiki's new all-white Tahoe truck and headed toward Auntie Mattie's house.

"I really like your knew truck," Justice complimented.

"Thanks. Clay got it for me. The Contour broke down one night on my way home from work. Clay trashed it the next day. He said he would not have me riding around in a car that's not dependable," Kiki smiled.

"Well, you deserve it. You have been riding in that car forever. But when I tried to buy you a car you almost had my head," Justice smiled going down memory lane.

"I know and I appreciate what you were trying to do. But you worked hard for your money. You shouldn't have to take care of me," Kiki explained.

"Well, I'm just glad Clay was able to talk you out of it," Justice laughed.

Inside the house Aunt Mattie was beside herself when she saw Justice. Justice gave her the pictures she had taken of her swearing in. She also had a picture framed for her aunt of her in her judge's robe sitting at her bench. Aunt Mattie cried for five straight minutes, and then finally she stopped.

"I am so proud of you." Aunt Mattie held her chest from excitement.

"I know, Auntie," Justice smiled.

"Oh, where is my head! Did you eat on that plane? Because I cooked a mess of food fer ya."

"No, I didn't eat because I knew you would cook."

"Well, come on to the kitchen." Aunt Mattie got off the couch.

They went into the kitchen where she had fried fish, greens, sweet potatoes, and fixed ice tea. Justice didn't pile her plate as usual, but she ate until she felt satisfied. She had missed her aunt's cooking, and this meal just showed her what good cooking she had to look forward to while she was home for a visit. She had even OK'd gaining a couple of pounds while she was home. She would work it off in the gym once she returned to New York. Justice had planned to go to her house that night after visiting with everyone. But after eating and talking for hours she decided to stay over with Aunt Mattie and Kiki.

Early the next morning Kiki woke her up. They had a busy day ahead. "Wake up, sleepyhead." Kiki had bounced down on Justice's old bed the way she used to when they were growing up.

"What time is it?" Justice rolled over wanting to go back to sleep.

"Eight o'clock."

"Just let me get a little more sleep." Justice attempted to pull the covers over her head.

"Oh no." Kiki pulled the covers down. "We have a long day. The wedding is tomorrow, remember? So the day starts now."

"What's on the agenda?" Justice sat up rubbing her face.

"Let's see, we have to pick up my dress. Get my hair and nails done. And the wedding rehearsal is tonight. Oh, and I know you are getting your hair done, right?"

"Yeah, I already made my appointment. So after we pick up your dress you can swing me by my house so I can check on things. Then I'll pick up my car and go to my appointment. And I'll see you tonight at the wedding rehearsal."

"Sounds like a plan to me. Now get out of bed." Kiki snatched the covers and they both started laughing.

"Calm down, married lady. I have to shower first."

"I know. I already brought your bags in." Kiki pointed toward the bags that she had placed on the floor next to the dresser in the corner.

Justice and Kiki arrived at Nina's Bridal two hours later to pick up her dress. When they stepped inside the store Justice was in awe of some of the dresses. They were absolutely beautiful. Kiki watched Justice looked around in amazement.

"It's hard to choose just one, right?" Kiki smiled.

"Yes. They are all beautiful."

"Hi, Kiki." Nina came from the back of the shop.

"I'm here to pick up my dress," Kiki beamed. "This is my cousin, Justice. She came all the way from New York. So this dress better knock her socks off," Kiki babbled.

"Hi, Justice." Nina reached out for a handshake.

"Hi, Nina," Justice said with a grin.

"Well, Justice get ready for your socks to be knocked off. I'll grab the dress." Nina headed toward the back. "Oh, go ahead and have a seat. I'll have Marcy bring you guys some wine." Nina signaled for her assistant to get in gear.

"Wine?" Justice whispered to Kiki. "At 10:30 A.M.?"

Marcy approached them with wineglasses. Both Justice and Kiki smiled. Neither of them planned to drink the wine. They would just hold the glasses to be polite.

Soon Nina came from the back with the most beautiful wedding dress Justice had ever seen. It was, without a doubt, a Vera Wang mermaid-style dress. It was an ivory strapless, side draped bodice with a cute asymmetrical neckline. Justice herself had dreamed of having a Vera Wang dress for her wedding. She knew that Kiki would be a knockout in the dress. She couldn't wait to see her in it.

"Isn't it beautiful?" Kiki said as she stood up to meet Nina.

"I love it, Kiki. Consider my socks knocked all the way off," Justice complimented in awe.

"Here is your dress. Vera Wang to the rescue. It flew in late last night, and I personally was at the airport waiting on it," Nina said with a grin as she placed the dress on a stand that had a hook so Kiki could admire the dress at full length.

"Kiki, I can't wait to see you in this." Justice was getting emotional.

"I can't wait to see me in this," Kiki smiled. "Whew," Kiki she said, then dabbed at a tear that was threatening to fall. "All right, Nina, you can wrap this up, and I will take it."

After safely placing the dress in the back of the Tahoe, Kiki headed toward Hedler's Hall where they would deliver the dress for the wedding. Hedler's Hall was beautiful. It was a country club in Gulfport. Clay had rented it for two days, which was no problem since he was a member. The whole wedding party would be staying there that night. Pulling into the club made Kiki tingle all over. Good things would be happening there that weekend, and she couldn't wait. Lives would be changed, people would walk happy and new.

ð374ð

The warmth hit Justice as soon as she opened the door to her house. She paused and took a look around. She looked up at the circular staircase and thought about how she used to run up those stairs after a long day at the office, craving her big four-poster Italian bed. Kiki stepped in around her and headed toward the kitchen. Kiki and Aunt Mattie had been looking in on the house for her, making sure everything was OK and the contractor kept the yard up.

"I'm thirsty. Think I'll grab myself a drink. You want something?" Kiki asked.

"No, I just want to look around." Justice headed toward the den.

"Have you heard anything from the realtor?" Kiki yelled from the kitchen.

"No, not yet. He's been showing it though." Justice yelled back just as Kiki entered drinking a bottled water.

"I'm sure it will sell soon."

"Yeah, I know." Justice said looking around. "Oh, you can show me your house while we are over here," Justice suggested. Kiki had informed Justice earlier that they would be moving a couple of houses down from her house. Clay had surprised her with the house a couple of weeks prior. Kiki was ecstatic.

After looking around her house making sure everything was still intact, the two friends drove down to look at Kiki's new house and Justice thought it was beautiful. Afterward, Justice had Kiki drop her back off at home so she could pick up her Benz so she wouldn't be late for her hair appointment. She couldn't wait to sit in her old beautician's chair again. Pepper had been doing Justice's hair for the last ten years. And true to her profession, Pepper didn't disappoint this time around. Her hair was off the chain for the wedding. She had it pinned up just as Kiki had requested. It was getting late so Justice said her good-byes after getting out of the chair and headed straight to Hedler's Hall.

When Justice pulled in she saw all the vehicles of everyone inside. It almost felt like the wedding day. Just the sight of Hedler's Hall with all those cars outside made her heart skip a beat with excitement because in less than twenty-four hours Kiki would be standing in front of the altar ready to say I do, forever. Justice couldn't help but wonder if she would ever get to that point, and her heart was filled with regret that she almost had it. All she had to do was say yes to Austin's proposal. She quickly threw her Benz into park fighting the urge to put it in drive and race straight over to his house. Not wanting to be late, though, she made her way inside the hall to the area where the wedding would be held.

"You finally made it." Kiki rushed over to Justice.

"Justice, Pepper has struck again! She does such a good job with your hair. I know you miss her," Kiki said, admiring Justice's look.

"I do, but I'll get over it. Besides, New York has every professional hairstylist you can name." Justice gave Kiki a slight smile. "But your hair is beautiful too. You are going to make a magnificent bride." Justice started to tear up.

"Now look." Kiki wiped at Justice's tears. "Don't start that cryin'. At least wait until tomorrow. Right now we need to rehearse." They both laughed as Kiki grabbed her hand and led the way.

"Hey, Justice," Clay spoke as he approached. "Why are you crying, Council?" Clay called Justice by his favorite word for her.

Justice dabbed at her eyes. "Those are happy tears, Clay. Just a little happiness," she smiled.

"All right. As long as you are not crying. Babe, when is rehearsal going to start? I'm getting hungry," he whined.

"Right now. I was just waiting on, Justice." Kiki took center stage so she could get everyone's attention. Her wedding planner came up behind her to assist.

"Places, everyone! Now remember, time is the most important word for tomorrow. If you are on time there is no way you can fall out of place." Kiki wagged her finger at everyone in the room.

Justice walked over to hug both her aunt Sylvia and aunt Mattie. The three of them smiled at Kiki and her instructions and expectations of them all. But none were shocked. Kiki always had a take-charge spirit. During the rehearsal for some reason Justice wasn't sure what it was, but she sort of felt like the rehearsal was centered around her. On many occasions she felt like bringing it to Kiki's attention but decided it was crazy. How could it be centered around her when it was Kiki's wedding? After two hours of rehearsal it finally came to a successful end.

The rehearsal party, that included family and friends, were all escorted to an exclusive rehearsal dinner where they ate, talked, and joked. And for the first time Justice got to meet Clay's mother and father, as well as other members of his family. They all seemed to love Kiki, but who wouldn't? She was a wonderful person. And Justice knew that her cousin, who had dated every loser Gulfport had to offer, had finally found her Mr. Right. So for the rest of the night Justice relaxed and enjoyed herself, but she seem to never

Saundra

take her eyes off the entrance, like she expected Austin to enter at any moment—but he never did.

ðð ð

Finally the wedding day arrived with an early rise and a delicious breakfast of fruit and pancakes. Justice and Kiki showered and started to prepare. People were coming from all over to see Kiki marry. It was indeed her day. Sitting at a table in the suite, Justice and Kiki had talked and laughed about some of Kiki's past dates.

"Well, that's enough about those losers." Justice couldn't stop laughing. "It's time for you to start getting ready. What time is the makeup artist supposed to be here? It's a must that your makeup be on point, no blemishes," Justice said matter-of-factly.

"He should be here any minute now," Kiki responded, drinking the last of her orange juice.

Just then someone knocked on the door. Justice jumped up to answer it.

"Hide! It may be Clay trying to get a glimpse of you." Justice waved Kiki toward the back of the suite.

"Justice, he knows better. Maybe it's the makeup artist," Kiki protested.

"Just hide, you never know," Justice insisted. Her mind was made up. She wouldn't open the door until Kiki was out of sight.

Kiki went into the hallway, and Justice slightly opened the door.

"Oh, Auntie, I thought you were Clay trying to get a peek at Kiki." Justice smiled at her Aunt Mattie who stepped inside the room.

"I was wondering what was taking you so long to answer."

"I told her, Auntie," Kiki said as she came back to the table.

"Not to worry about the men. They are on the other side of the courtyard with their own country club view. Besides, your aunt Sylvia is standing guard," Aunt Mattie laughed.

Then there was another knock. Justice opened the door to find the makeup artist and his crew ready to begin.

"Hi, I thought there would only be one of you," Justice said as she studied them.

"We travel in packs," Martin, the lead makeup artist, spoke up with a grin.

"Well, come on in. They're here," Justice informed Kiki over her shoulder.

"So who is the beautiful bride?" Martin used his charm.

"She is." Justice pointed to Kiki with a smile.

"Are you ready for Martin to work his magic and make you even more beautiful?" he asked.

"I sure am. And this is the other person I spoke of. I want you to make her beautiful. Remember what we discussed over the phone?" Kiki nodded at Martin.

"Sure, dear, Martin never forgets."

"Justice, I want you to be made up by the artist as well."

"No, that won't be necessary. I'll do mine. You know I do a good job." Justice was almost an artist herself when it came to her makeup which she wore little of most of the time.

"Justice, will you do this for me? It's supposed to be *my* day, remember?" Kiki pouted to get her way.

"OK." Justice gave in. She decided to not protest any further. She would make Kiki happy on her wedding day.

"Now, Martin, you can do her makeup," Kiki pointed toward Justice.

Martin gave Kiki a smile and ordered Justice to his space where he had set up his equipment.

"Kiki, Martin is here to do *you*." Justice seemed confused.

"Justice, it does not matter. Now sit. Martin's professionals will take care of me." Kiki pointed to the other two artists that had come along with him.

"OK, whatever. Let's just get this on the road. I will not be the reason you are late walking down the aisle." Justice looked to her aunt for an answer, but there was none.

It took two hours of makeup before both ladies looked like they were supermodels about to hit the runway. There was not a blemish visible on either one of them. Martin and his crew had packed up and ascended to the chapel to be seated for the wedding which they had undeniably been invited to as well. Just after they left the room there was a tap at the door. Kiki answered and was told that it was time for them to come down to the dressing room where the bride and maid of honor would be getting dressed.

Pacing slowly behind Kiki who seemed to be taking her time getting to the dressing room, Justice opened the door to find Austin standing in the middle of the room. To say she was shocked was an understatement. Her tongue was tied as she turned to Kiki for answers. But Kiki had swiftly shut the door and made a clean getaway.

"Hi," was the only word Justice let nervously slip from her lips.

"Hey." Austin looked her dead in her eyes.

Shifting her legs, to an upward position it took every ounce of strength in Justice's body not to run to him. She had missed him tremendously. But now was not the time to show weakness.

"How have you been?" Justice tried to break the ice.

"I've been good." Austin responded.

Justice had no idea of what to say next. She felt closed in.

"But I have been thinking a lot about us. About our future together. I can't let you go. No, let me rephrase that. I *won't* let you go."

"Austin, we have already talk—" Austin cut her off.

"I know what we discussed in the past, and that's not working. I love you, Justice, and my heart goes where you go. When you board that plane back to New York, I will be on it."

Justice felt defeated. There was nothing she could say. He had laid the ground rules. "What about your job? What about Morgan?" Justice asked, not sure of what else to say. She had no fight.

"I have already taken care of that. I will be heading up that division I told you about. And Morgan, she can't wait to move. She'll be closer to her grandma Tess. So after we return from our honeymoon, Morgan will make the flight out to New York to be with us."

Justice's mind stopped working at *honeymoon*. "What honeymoon?"

"Justice, will you marry me?" Austin got down on one knee.

Tears flooded her face as she, without hesitation, accepted. "Yes, yes. I will marry you." Austin picked her up and spun her around planting kisses all over her face.

"I have one more thing to ask you. Will you marry me *today?*"

"Austin, we can't. This is Kiki's wedding day. I can't do that to her." Justice shook her head.

"Actually, no. This is *your* wedding day. Kiki is not getting married until tomorrow. I rented the hall for today, and Clay rented it for tomorrow. All of this is for you, including that Vera Wang dress that you always dreamed of."

Justice threw her arms around Austin's neck. "She told you, didn't she?" Justice cried.

"Yes, she did," Austin grinned. Kiki had picked that dress for Justice because only she knew how much Justice dreamed of getting married in a Vera Wang dress.

Now it all made sense to Justice—the dress, the wedding rehearsal being centered around her, and the makeup. It all made sense they had planned this without her knowing a thing.

A knock at the door cut Justice's thoughts short. Kiki opened the door and looked directly at Austin. "Did she say yes?"

"Of course, she said yes." Austin was modest. The grin on his face was priceless.

"Remind me to kill you later," Justice joked. Giving Kiki a fake threatening look.

"At least wait until this is over. Now you two have to hurry and get dressed. It's almost time. And a wedding can't start without a bride and groom. Austin, go get into your tux," Kiki ordered him.

With Kiki and Aunt Mattie's help, Justice got into her dress that fit her perfectly. And after admiring herself in the mirror, she waved Kiki out of the room so she could prepare for her own stroll down the aisle as her maid of honor, Kiki, gave her a wink before exiting the room. Aunt Mattie got in place to walk Justice down the aisle.

Justice couldn't believe that Kiki and her aunt had thought of everything, even the three most important parts of a wedding for a girl—something borrowed, new, and blue. For something borrowed, Aunt Mattie had given Justice her mother's engagement ring. Justice's eyes lit up in amazement when Aunt Mattie pulled out the ring.

Justice reached for the ring as if it were a child she would love and care for. "Oh my God, Auntie. Where did you get this? The last time I saw her she had it on," Justice said, referring to her mother.

"The military sent it to me, along with her possessions. So I put it up for you. I promised myself that I would give it to you on your wedding day."

Justice slid the ring on her finger next to the pinkie on her left hand. She admired it on her finger. "It's a perfect fit. Thank you sooo much, Auntie." Justice gave her a huge hug.

"It's all right, baby. Now you stop that crying before you ruin your makeup. Besides, here is something new and something blue." Aunt Mattie handed her the items in her hand.

Kiki had purchased her a baby blue Prada garter for something blue. And last but not least, her aunt Mattie gave her a diamond cut tennis bracelet. Justice said a little silent prayer as walked toward the entrance that would lead her down the aisle. Then out of the blue "Here and Now" by the Luther Vandross "here and now" blasted out of the speakers. Aunt Mattie smiled as she clasped Justice's hand, and they strolled down the aisle.

Walking down the aisle Justice was nervous until she started to see all the familiar smiling faces. On the right there was Tabitha, who already had tears streaming down her cheeks. Then she saw Candice standing with Brian giving her a thumbs-up with a grin. And all around were her family who she loved dearly. But she felt like someone was missing. She searched the audience for Morgan, who she didn't see anywhere in sight. But her heart skipped a beat when she made it to the front and saw Morgan standing beside Kiki looking as beautiful as ever. Justice stepped over and gave her a kiss on the cheek.

Then, ready to make her acquaintance was Austin, who outstretched his hand and took both her hands into his. With tears and a smile on his face, Austin led Justice back to the spot where they would stand to exchange their vows. Trent stood behind Austin, giving Justice a reassuring smile. Reverend Diddimore graciously recited their wedding vows to them while on purpose leaving out "obey" upon Austin's request.

"I now with great pleasure introduce to you—Mr. and Mrs. Crews," Reverend Diddimore smiled.

Austin pulled Justice in for a long, passionate kiss. For a moment he forgot all about the crowd that was sitting there observing them. But the crowd didn't disappoint them as a host of their family and friends started to clap. They both stopped kissing and turned around to jump the broom which had been laid out by Kiki upon Aunt Mattie's request.

Chapter Twenty-Four

One Year Later

Justice had been watching for the gate to open because she couldn't wait for Aunt Mattie and Kiki to arrive. Austin had left over two hours ago to pick them up from the airport. But her feet had started to hurt so she could no longer wait, and she was dehydrated so she yelled for Morgan to bring her something to drink. For someone reason she was constantly thirsty. She wondered if all of her fluids were being sucked dry.

Just then she heard Austin put his key in the door. Justice stood as fast as was achievable for her. She and Kiki embraced first as soon as they met in the entryway.

"Look at you. You are so beautiful." Kiki reached down and rubbed Justice's bulging stomach. Kiki and Aunt Mattie had decided to come out for a visit since the baby was due any day now. Dr. Shapiro had released Aunt Mattie to travel over six months ago since her health had improved so much. There were no bad signs at all. She took all of her medicine on time and had been working out with the personal trainer that Justice had acquired and still paid for her. So she and Kiki had decided this would be the perfect time to visit. Kiki had taken a three-week vacation from Walmart, and they had hit the airport headed for New York. They would stay until Justice had the baby, and then a week or so after. Aunt Mattie had bugged Kiki on the whole flight over that Justice was probably in labor while they were in the air and that they would miss the birth. But Kiki had assured her over and over again that Justice would hold the baby's schedule up until they arrived. And now they were in New York inside the house, and Aunt Mattie had a front-row seat to her first great-grandnephew.

Aunt Mattie looked at Justice and instantly started to cry. "Don't cry, Auntie." Justice reached out for a huge hug. "It's a happy time." Justice rubbed her stomach with one hand, and the baby kicked right on cue. "See, feel here. That kick was just for you. It was a welcome kick," Justice smiled.

"Baby, these are happy tears," Aunt Mattie assured her. "I just can't believe you are having a baby. I can't wait to be a great-aunt." Aunt Mattie dabbed at her tears with her hands until Austin came up behind her and handed her a handkerchief. "Now where is that beautiful Morgan?" Aunt Mattie had missed her.

"I'm right behind you," Morgan said. She had crept up behind Aunt Mattie as she wiped her tears away.

"Hi, baby."

Morgan reached out for a handshake. But she was only kidding. She knew Aunt Mattie would insist on a hug. Morgan remembered the very first time she had met Aunt Mattie she had made her an instant part of her family. She would never forget that.

Saundra

Aunt Mattie gave her a strange look that was full of love. "You better come here and give me a hug." She embraced Morgan as tight as she could. "You still beautiful as ever."

"Thanks." Morgan blushed. Since she had been in school in New York she had been offered several modeling jobs but had declined them all until lately. She decided to do a few commercial shoots with her dad's approval, hich actually paid her really good money, and she put it all into her bank account. But she didn't want to make a career out of it. She had planned to be a judge someday, just like Justice.

Justice stood back and watched Aunt Mattie interact with Morgan. It warmed her heart to know that Morgan would have Aunt Mattie in her life. Someone who would love her until the end of time the same way she had loved her.

"So Clay couldn't make it, huh" Justice inquired.

"Nope. He has that trial where the mother is accused of drowning her kids," Kiki released. "He really wanted to come. He told me to apologize to you both. And he wants me to assure you that we both will be back in the spring," Kiki informed them.

"Kiki, would you please tell him not to sweat it. We totally understand. Just because I'm a judge does not mean I forgot how the trial courts can be."

"I told him a thousand times you would understand. I see you moved all the way out into the sticks. What happened to the penthouse? I mean, this mansion is nice and all, but I thought I would be twelve floors up for a couple of days." Kiki looked around admiring the house from her spot.

"I'm sorry, Kiki." Justice smiled at her. "We moved here about six months ago. Austin and I decided that this would be a better place to raise Morgan and the baby. Besides, the city is too noisy. You can hardly get any sleep. How would I raise a baby in a traffic jam?" Justice joked. "But don't worry, I'll take you into the city every day while you're here. We'll shop until you drop."

"That is, if you don't drop first." Kiki rubbed Justice's huge belly.

"Yep, the doctor says any day now, so the walking will do me good because I am ready to get him out of here." Justice referred to the baby. She had had an ultrasound a couple of weeks ago, and the doctor had confirmed it was a boy. She and Austin had already decided on the name Augstin.

"And don't forget that you promised to introduce me to P. Diddy while I'm here. So get him on the phone, ASAP," Kiki demanded.

Justice thought about all that had transpired for her in the past starting with Keith's shocking betrayal. Then her meeting Austin and successfully gaining full custody of Morgan for him. She also reminisced on Austin's fly-by-minute proposal that she had painfully turned down and continued with her original plan to move across the country to New York. Then her Prince Charming Austin's planning and pulling off not only his proposal to her, but arranging their entire wedding with the help of her family, without her knowledge, making her, without a doubt, the happiest woman the world. She was also very proud of Morgan who embraced New York so much since moving there. Morgan had openheartedly welcomed her grandma Tess back into her life as well as joining a swim team and winning first place in a national swim contest. And even taken on modeling, which had shocked Justice and Austin. Justice had a lot to be proud of, but most of all, her new family.

Yes, the last past year had been extremely hard for her with all her situations. So much so that Justice, at one point, felt the only thing she had to look forward to was her job. She had all but given up on having her own family once she moved to New York.

But Austin had not taken no for an answer. And he had come back into her life and showed her the way back to love. A slow love even without intention. He had shown her that it takes time to be in love, but ultimately, in the end, it was worth it. She was living proof of that. Not only did she have a loving husband and a beautiful stepdaughter, but love had planted itself inside of her and set the stage to cultivate into something that would motivate all of her actions from then forward.

Discussion Questions

1.   Justice relationship with Keith ended because of his deliberate lie and deception of being engaged to marry someone else. What do you think was his true intention with Justice since he was engaged to her at the same time?

2.   Kiki and Aunt Mattie goal was to make sure Justice finds love. Do they believe if she finds love this will fill the void of Keith?

3.   Austin clearly fell in love with Justice the first time he bumped into her at the court house. And although kept trying to convince himself hat would respect their attorney slash client relationship. Was it ever a chance he could consciously do that? Or was he wasting his time trying because he couldn't contain himself around her?

4.   Morgan despised and rejected Justice in the beginning because she knew her father liked her. Was the rejection of Justice and abandonment issue Morgan felt because of her mom continuing to walk out of her life? Or did Morgan feel threatened that her father would love her less if Justice was in the picture?

5.   Kiki dated one loser guy after the other it was repeated pattern. However, when Clay a successful attorney approached her she didn't understand why he would want to date her. Did Kiki have a hidden self esteem probablem? Was that self esteem problem the reason she attracted or was attracted to loser guys?

6.   After Austin and Justice share a passionate night together he confesses his love over lunch only to have Justice tell him she has been offered a job as a judge in New York.

Austin Proposes to Justice when she officially tells him she is leaving but she turns him down. According to Justice she didn't want to move Morgan away from her newly secured life with Austin. But was Justice trying to protect her own heart this time around? Did she have flash backs of Keith and the way their engagement ended? Did she think this hurt could happen yet again?

7.   Austin planned his wedding for himself and Justice without her knowing anything about it. Did he ever consider there was a chance she would turn him down twice? How could he be so sure she loved him? Because remember Justice kept her love for him guarded.

8.   Will Justice and Austin love sustain the test of time? How deep really was their love for one another? Because they both had heart break from relationships past.

Also Available in stores

{ DELPHINE PUBLICATIONS PRESENTS }

The HOLY City

MICHAEL F BLAKE

Cookie Too
LYRIC'S SONG

A NOVEL BY **DEE SHANA** &
TAMIKA NEWHOUSE
AUTHOR OF *COOKIE*